MW00569200

Fireships & Brimstone

Joe Gaspe Defends the North Coast

RICHARD A. MINICH

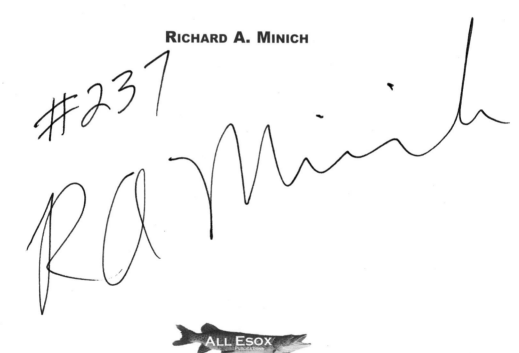

#237

RA Minich

ALL ESOX
PUBLICATIONS
RICHARD MINICH

Copyright 2007 by Richard A. Minich. All rights reserved.
No part of this document may be reproduced by any means,
mechanical, electronic, digital, or otherwise, without
the expressed written permission of the author.

ISBN: 9780975872819

Library of Congress Control Number: 2007904240

All Esox Publications
P.O. Box 493
East Aurora, NY 14052

www.AllEsoxPublications.com

Artwork by: Susan Nowak – cover
Patricia A. Lanigan Eberle – portraiture
Theresa Meegan – oyarons

Book Design by Janice Phelps (www.janicephelps.com)

To Mark Treu
Friend, Fisherman, Partner, Rest In Peace

Acknowledgments

Thanks to my book designer Janice Phelps who does a great job and somehow fits my schedule into hers. Thanks to my three artists, Sue Nowak, Pat Eberle and Theresa Meegan, all worked without a net.

I received invaluable assistance from four critical readers; Cheryl Morrisey, who wasn't shy about telling me what to do differently, Rick Jackson, who contributed a fisherman's perspective, Dave McCuen, for a non-fisherman, voracious reader's outlook, and Dr. Mick Stern, an old friend with an academic outlook.

Additional advice and encouragement were provided by pre-readers Cheryl Mediak and Chris Zeth. Thanks.

The ideas for some of the hi-jinks were extrapolated from Tales of Treu as told by Jim Reynolds.

Thanks to my wife Joan and my daughter Holly for putting up with a grouch who does little besides read, write, work, and fish.

*Then the Lord rained upon Sodom and Gomorrah
brimstone and fire from the Lord out of heaven*

Genesis 19: 24

Fireships & Brimstone

Joe Gaspe Defends the North Coast

Joe Gaspe

Prologue

June 16th

"The dead Oriental guy is up above on the dam." Tribal Police Chief Leonard Brant was leaning in the window of Agent Thomas Andre's white Chevy Suburban.

"He's Asian, Leonard; rugs are oriental, and people are Asian." The Assistant Special Agent in Charge of the FBI Office in Pantherville knew the Chief from conferences and meetings but he had never been on this part of the Rez before.

"Whatever. He's dead and he's not of the people." Chief Brant turned and walked across the gravel road to where the trickle of water from the dam spilled out and passed through a culvert under the road.

The slightly built FBI agent walked up beside the imposing Iroquois policeman and followed his gaze. They were about sixty feet away from, and fifteen feet lower in elevation than, a partially buried corpse laid out as if he'd been crucified.

Thomas Andre looked into the grayish dead face of his unofficial agent–special asset Derek Chang. There were seven specific reasons why the federal police agency could establish jurisdiction on tribal lands. Murder of a federal agent certainly qualified. An invitation from the tribal council to cooperate with the reservation police made the FBI agent's presence doubly acceptable.

"The beavers buried him to stop the flow through the dam. Whoever did this knocked part of the dam apart in the process of displaying their kill," Chief Brant said. A State Trooper with the name Oleniczak on his shirtfront joined agent Andre. "Beavers hate the sound of running water and will work until they're done to plug a leak in the dam."

"Do you suppose he's an illegal who didn't pay up?" Trooper Oleniczak asked.

"We'll have to investigate all possibilities. Do you have forensics people here?" Agent Andre was cautious about procedures and inter-department politics.

"Yeah, they just arrived. I'll see that they do a thorough job." Trooper Oleniczak averred.

Agent Andre went back to his car and removed his expensive slip-on shoes, pulled on some low cut L.L.Bean boots, and re-crossed the dirt road thinking, "I wonder if there are any dirt roads in this state other than on the Indian lands."

"Take me over there for a closer look, please, Chief Brant."

"This is my case. I can just send you some photos of the crime scene," Trooper Oleniczak said, looming between Brant and Andre. Agent Andre had been tucking his trouser leg inside his boot when he heard that. He froze. Chief Brant made a little noise halfway between urf and woof. Andre rose up and, at five seven, one hundred forty pounds, he stared down the six-foot two-inch two hundred twenty pound Trooper. Brant had seen this before: Andre, slight, soft-spoken, and unusually polite for the twenty first century, had a steel backbone and could dredge up a look so cold and piercing it would freeze anyone.

"The Federal Government will oversee your case. You can handle it in your usual exemplary manner with full reports on my desk every twenty-four hours and phone calls if urgent information warrants. Now Chief Brant and I are going to have a look at your DOA." The authority of the small black man went unchallenged by the hulking white State Trooper.

They reached the top of the dam and were looking down and slightly west. The dam held back a pond of ten acres. A slight south-westerly breeze rippled the surface. The top of the dam was wide enough for a lawnmower or garden tractor but neither wide enough nor strong enough for a pick-up or an SUV.

"Who found the body?"

"Charley Potts' twin ten-year-old boys. Actually, it was their dog, Oscar. They were catching frogs down below and the dog must have smelled it." He said this with a tilt of his head toward the dead man.

"Anything of interest obviously left behind?"

"You ask that like you expect something."

"I do. The way he is displayed, like a crucifixion, someone wanted him found, perhaps not right away, but his position sends a message."

"Oh, I get it. Christians, keep out. You think it's one of mine that did this?"

"Actually Leonard," Agent Andre slipped into and out of the familiar form of address according to whether or not they were alone, "I don't think the Rez is anything more than an out-of-the-way place in this case. Have there been any non-residents observed, other than commercial visitors?" At this, Trooper Oleniczak came crashing and puffing through the brush to join them.

He was red in the face when he said, "There's so many folks buying smokes and gas, who could tell who belonged or not."

"We notice unusual activity. Your killers left that garden rake behind. There are tracks from a lawn tractor with a trailer in the tall grass along here."

"I saw those, and the drag marks to the slope— marks that would be gone in a week if the grass was mowed or grew a little longer, one."

Chief Brant ignored the trooper and spoke directly to Agent Andre. "Joseph Smokes pulled a landscape truck and trailer out of a ditch three miles from here. Unusual crew in the van, though."

"What was unusual about them?" asked Oleniczak

"Joseph said the white man was an ordinary, flat-headed, ugly white, but the others in the truck were not young whites, but two Orientals. Big Orientals with smooth hands."

"These Asian gentleman did not seem like typical landscapers, eh?" Agent Andre stressed the descriptive term "Asian" for Leonard's benefit and because the Trooper was present.

"Joseph said they didn't speak English but jabbered at each other and on a cell phone in what he took to be Chinese."

"Did the landscaping company's name appear on the equipment?"

"It did. But Joseph can no longer read."

Returning to his vehicle, Andre wondered who he'd find to replace Derek Chang. Then he had an idea.

Chapter 1

May 3rd

"Joe, we're being tailed by a boat, a big boat, are we cool?" Marv was looking back to watch the rods while Joe looked forward to be precise on the trolling run.

"We're good. Is it the Coast Guard, DEC, what?"

"Too big to be DEC. I thought they didn't even have a boat. It's got to be Coast Guard and it's not their little patrol boat, this one's at least thirty-two feet."

"Whadda they doin'?"

"They are about one hundred yards back and to the port side and they have been matching our speed for the last few minutes."

Seven weeks before musky fishing season opens on the Musky Straits, the official start of warm water fishing season begins with the opening day of walleye and pike fishing, on the first Saturday in May. There is also a restricted early season for smallmouth bass opening that day, and there were early season boaters out as well. Marv Ankara and Joe Gaspe were making their first trip of the season to the Upper Lake at Pantherville Harbor, to fish for pike. They wouldn't be all that sad if they picked up a nice musky or two during the outing. As was their custom, they had planned the trip for a Monday evening when the waters would be less crowded than on the opening weekend.

Joe and Marv are construction workers and, as such, they work most Saturdays. Every once in awhile they get sick for a day of fishing. Marv, a roofer, single and serially semi-attached, is five-seven, stocky, with light brown hair. He has an open, weathered face and a dreamy expression. He was soured on education in first grade by being labeled hyperactive, a euphemism the school systems had begun using in his generation for "behaves like a boy." His fishing partner Joe Gaspe had been his friend since high school when they had shared the adventures of youth. Joe has a football lineman's build, six feet tall with a long torso, short powerful legs and a big sturdy butt. He fights a weight problem because he indulges his prodigious appetites for food, drink, and other pleasures. He has a big head of coarse hair, a moustache, and a pair of penetrating, arresting eyes. He can turn his gaze from the lasers of a hawk to the Irish twinkle of a lady-killer, at will.

They were in Joe's 14 foot Smoker Craft with a forty horse power Evinrude outboard, had their smorgasbord of snacks laid out in the center, and were trolling a familiar pattern.

Joe had a few compound turns to make in order to swing his trolled lures onto and off of the weed lines marked by the channel buoys. He wasn't doing anything unlawful and as long as he wasn't risking collision, he didn't plan on altering his track along one of the best pike fishing runs in Pantherville Harbor. When he got to a straightaway part he glanced over his left shoulder and saw the cutter following. It was staying in the position most difficult for him to monitor while driving his fishing boat.

The sky was low and gray, spitting a light drizzle on this Monday evening and Joe and Marv were the only anglers out in the north end of Pantherville Harbor. To catch a Northern Pike, they fished their usual musky runs. They just fished more shallowly with a smaller lure and trolled more slowly. Cruising against the waves from buoy number one to the end of Dennehey's wall, Joe was startled to see a second Coast Guard boat, the twenty-two foot patrol boat, flash across his bow, at planing speed. It swooped around behind him and roared down the line of bubbles he had left in his wake.

"That son of a bitch was close, doesn't he know the rules of the road?" Joe thought Marv sounded jumpy. Before he could answer, a low-flying helicopter set up a terrible racket as it swooped in, tracking backwards along the patrol boat's path. The cutter maintained its distance, just far enough back that Joe had to turn completely around to see it.

"What the hell is going on?" Marv was scared and ticked off at the same time.

"If they want us to stop, they'll do something to let us know," Joe said. He noticed that two P-3 Orion sub-chasing airplanes had just come over the Friendship Bridge and were headed his way. one thousand feet above.

The Smoker Craft cleared the south end of Dennehey's and headed behind the north end of the short wall with all four lines working their lures well. The patrol boat had turned around in the ship canal, pegged its twin 185 Honda outboards, and raced back on its previous track. The helo that had turned parallel to and above Dennehey's Wall turned sharply to the west and headed straight for the Smoker Craft. The world was closing in on Joe and Marv. The patrol boat became mouse quiet as it flashed up from behind; its four stroke outboards were quieter than electric pencil sharpeners. The helicopter battered the air with its roaring, chopping, noisy pressure wave. It came in low enough for its rotor to pick up spray from the wave tips. The two P-3s droned above, passing right over the gap between walls where Joe's boat was crossing the open water.

To change the game, Joe decided to scrape as close to the back end of the short wall as he could. This would force the cutter to peel off and make the patrol boat switch to an overtaking course on the starboard side. He couldn't do anything about the aircraft.

Joe keyed the microphone on his marine radio.

"Coast Guard, Pantherville, Coast Guard Pantherville, this is Dr. Dento, do you copy?" Joe was on channel 16, the emergency channel on the VHF radio.

"Go ahead Doctor, this is Coast Guard Pantherville."

"Yes, I'm in the north end of Pantherville Harbor and I am being pursued by unidentified vessels and harassed by a helicopter pilot who must be nuts. I request assistance."

"Sorry, Doctor, this is Coast Guard Pantherville, I didn't copy that."

Before he keyed the mike again, Joe looked to his left. The Coast Guard station, situated on the north end of Pantherville harbor, was less than one mile away. He knew they heard him. He looked at Marv, who was lighting one cigarette off the end of another.

"Lying bastards," said Marv.

"Private vessel Doctor Dento, please repeat last transmission, do you copy?" This was the Coast Guard again.

Joe keyed the mike, thought about what to say and looked around. The cutter had pulled off going south along the short wall. Instead of coming around that wall to take another run at Joe and Marv, it headed south down the harbor. The helicopter had regained altitude and turned east toward the city of Pantherville. The P-3s, having taken a big lazy turn, were headed back upriver to the Musky Falls airbase at the Cascades. The patrol boat was idling its twin squirrels about a quarter mile off Joe's starboard bow. He put the mike down.

"Private vessel Doctor Dento, please move to channel twenty-one, do you copy?"

Joe looked at Marv, "They scared the crap out of us on a training mission." He knew now that the Smoker Craft had been a target for tactical training and that his call to the Coast Guard had ended the war game.

"We don't look like terrorists. What the hell are they doing?"

"Look around, Marv, there is no other boat available. I'd guess they had an exercise on the schedule and all they had to work on was us."

"Oughta sue the bastards."

"C'mon Marv, you saw what happened on 9/11. We were doing our part for homeland security. At least now we'll have something exciting to talk about."

Joe's run had now taken him into a big 180-degree turn to give the end of Dennehey's another good scrape. The cutter was lost to sight in the misty drizzle. The smaller Patrol Craft still loomed but they seemed occupied with shipboard tasks. The aircraft were all gone. Joe and Marv settled down to some serious pike fishing.

Putt, putt, pfffttt. The motor quit. "We're outta gas, I'll change tanks." Marv was on it.

"Uh, the other tank's empty too. I changed 'em in the driveway before we left home."

"Well, we can get gas at the upper end marina."

"Uh, they closed at six o'clock.

"Well, genius, what the hell do we do?"

"Let's bring in the lines first." Joe was going to have to think of something.

The screen door to the CPO's (Chief Petty Officer) Club was one that would hit you in the butt as it slammed. Closed by a spring instead of a hydraulic cylinder, it allowed entry into a martial and nautical realm that was big enough to accommodate two hundred more people than the two who occupied it at present. A big ruddy-faced man sat at the long polished wooden bar. He was faced by a crisp bartender, a man trim in haircut and overdressed, in a conservative and high quality manner, for his task.

Joe had been faced with two choices of where to beg for gas when he paddled the last few yards to the east side of Red Rock canal. He could try the American Yacht Club where dinner was in progress and every moored boat was big enough for Joe's Smoker Craft to be its tender, or he could try the CPO club with its unimposing weather-beaten two-story exterior. That club had a sign across the wall facing the water. The sign read, *Pantherville CPO Club*, and below that in smaller letters, "*We welcome NCOs (Non-Commissioned Officers) from all branches of service, for the USA and our allies, past or present.*"

Well, the Mohawks had been US allies on and off over the centuries. And Joe's mother and stepmother were Mohawks. Though the Yacht Club had a gas dock, it also had a dress code and signs all along its frontage that said, "Members Only, All Guests <u>Must</u> Register with the Commodore."

Joe walked quickly to the bar next to the lone patron and responded, "I'll have a Blue," when the bartender asked. He introduced himself to the man at the bar and found that he was talking to Bill Cote, a man of contrasts.

Cote was six feet tall and weighed about two seventy. Instead of the hard muscle of a military man he had the soft body of an office worker. A former gunnery sergeant in the Marines, he'd been a securities attorney for twenty years. Over his second pink wine cooler he told Joe that he was treasurer of the CPO Club and had held that office since the Board of Directors discovered that they could dragoon him into straightening out their financial and legal affairs.

"Bill, do you know anyplace we can get gas for our outboard around here? My partner Marv is with the boat and we don't have enough gas to get down to the boat launch where we left the truck and trailer."

"Zeke, bring me that phone if you will, please."

The bartender brought a cordless phone to Bill Cote who turned to Joe and said, "I'll have Commodore Richards send a boy over with five gallons. He's a former client of mine. He owes me a few favors."

Joe couldn't believe his luck. Cote got his call to the Yacht Club put through to the appropriate party. The screen door slammed again and Joe did a double take. There was Mel Dumke—the guy he'd bought most of his musky gear from—hurrying to the restroom.

Joe settled up with the bartender for his beer and Bill Cote's wine cooler. Joe had been trying not to listen to Cote's phone conversation when he turned to Joe and asked, "Where is your boat now?"

"We're tied to that PT boat down alongside your dock."

"WHAT!!? Get that boat away from there! Immediately! Before you are arrested!"

Joe looked at Cote and Zeke the bartender. They both made it obvious with their expressions and stiff body language that he'd tied his boat in the wrong place. He wasn't sure why, but it was a bad thing he and Marv had done.

Joe took off for the door and noticed Mel Dumke coming out of the little hallway to the restrooms, looking around at the commotion. Joe ran down the lawn toward the little club dock and saw that Marv was in trouble with more guys than one little roofer could handle.

Marv was talking and gesticulating at the Coast Guard Patrol Boat where an Officer, with a loud hailer, was shouting at him from fifteen feet away. Meanwhile two uniformed men with drawn sidearms were climbing across the PT boat—a museum piece moored to the CPO club dock—in order to reach Marv and take him down.

The Officer on the Coast Guard boat said, "Put your hands in the air and do not move from where you are."

Marv had been heating up some pork and beans in a can in the center of the Smoker Craft. He had boiled the can over, spilling some beans onto the burner, creating a large smoke cloud. Shaking with fear, he did as the Coast Guard Officer said.

Into this mayhem came three people; Joe Gaspe running from the club—about forty yards—hollering and waving his arms, a teenage boy in a too-big muscle shirt with a head full of floppy hair, wheeling a cart with a five gallon gas can, and behind these two was Mel Dumke blowing a ship's whistle and double timing it to the scene of the confrontation.

Joe was able to mentally slow time down in a crisis. He could observe things happening quickly and all around as if they were separate items. The two armed men, apparently security for the CPO club, stopped immediately, when the ship's whistle sounded. They kept their guns on Marv, but looked in Dumke's direction. The Coast Guard crew observed Joe's approach, at running speed, and turned their attention and weapons on him. The teenager, listening to something very loud on his headphones, was watching his loaded cart as it bumped over the lawn, and neither saw nor heard anything as he strolled into the mayhem.

"You, there on the lawn, STOP! Do not come any closer." This was the loud hailer directed at Joe. The CPO security officers switched their weapons from Marv to Joe to the gas dock boy and back. Joe stopped and raised his hands in surrender. The oblivious kid kept approaching. Joe heard the screen door slam again.

Mel Dumke blew his whistle one more time and the security men lowered their weapons. Bill Cote had come onto the lawn now and was limping down toward the boats behind Dumke. The gas boy continued to watch his load in the cart and jive to his tunes while treading the path between the Yacht Club and the CPO club. Only Joe and Marv were not moving now.

In the next five minutes, the crisis passed. Dumke called off his security guards, Bill Cote jawboned the Coast Guard Patrol into continuing on their way, paid the boy from the yacht club for gas, and supervised Joe's boat moving down the canal to a legal mooring while the fuel was loaded. Joe thanked Mel Dumke, sergeant-at-arms of the CPO club, and Bill Cote treasurer, and he and Marv were able to cast off with sufficient fuel.

"That was wild. But I have a stupid suggestion," said Joe.

"What's that?"

"Want to do some pike fishing."

Unaffected by their near misses with The Department of Homeland Security, pike fishing is what they did.

Dr. Marie Bramton was hot with fury when she smacked Joe Gaspe in the back of the head. It was unprofessional behavior in the examining room but she had had enough of his antics. Later she would have second thoughts about where she'd landed her blow. She knew his face and ears were vulnerable, she'd recently worked on his chest, and his back was going under the knife in a few minutes. She had taken the moment, after her nurse left the room, to let Joe know she was tired of his misbehavior. At five foot two, Dr.Marie was attractive and shapely, yet she packed quite a wallop. Before the nurse returned, she let loose with a verbal barrage aimed at her best friend's husband.

"When are you going to stop being such a jerk? You have five kids and a wife at home and you treat yourself like you're some nineteen-year-old punk. I've got other things to do besides work on you and your latest medical disaster. You need to take care of yourself like you're a husband and a father." She paused.

"Oh Joe! I love you, but you're such a mess. Look at this chart! You've got a record of injuries long enough for six men. You've been seriously burned in the upper body, slightly burned in the hand and arm, beaten savagely by several men, and now for the second time, you've been caught with a huge fishhook. Not only that, but each time you hooked yourself, you kept fishing for hours before coming in to have the hook removed! You jackass! When I endorsed you taking up fishing, I told Kate it would be better than hanging around bars with your construction worker buddies. I felt pity for you when you got the crap beat out of you just for smiling at the wrong girl in a bar, but that lovable rogue act of yours works too well sometimes. That time I should have written a diagnosis for facial injuries as 'all busted up.' Then, you skipped your court date to testify against those thugs in order to go fishing, and they skated!" Dr Bramton was winding down as her assistant returned.

Nurse Gruery was a country girl who had worked at the private Muskedaigua Clinic for only a few weeks and she had never met Gaspe before. He was that kind of slightly dangerous guy who, while not handsome or wealthy, still manages to charm the girls with the twinkle in his eye and his offhand friendly manner. He was effortlessly winning her over as she admired his courage and ability to withstand pain because Dr. Marie's treatment seemed a lot rougher than normal.

The Muskedaigua Clinic was just a small country office. That is why Dr. Bramton always seemed to be the one working on Joe. Gaspe showed up at the clinic with a stub of a huge treble hook embedded in his back under his right shoulder blade. His fishing partner, Marv Ankara, had cut off the hook and removed the giant musky lure leaving just the barbed part in Joe's back.

"We were trying for a personal best. I'd seen that fish up close. She was hot, had made a good follow on a shallow lure and Marv was going to throw back with a topwater when he caught me on his back cast. It didn't hurt that much. It was only gonna be a little while."

"Just shut up, Joe! You waited four hours and drove ninety miles with a dirty fishhook in you." Dr. Bramton refused the nurse's proffered syringe of local anesthetic as she cut away the last of the fabric of Gaspe's sweatshirt, flannel shirt, and undershirt. The Doctor grabbed the stub of the hook and pushed it back through the skin of Joe's back. Because the barbs resist removal by backing them out, fishhooks are usually removed by pushing them out through the skin. Occasionally, pushing through doesn't work and they have to be surgically removed with an incision. The nurse set aside the anesthetic as Joe gasped and held his breath for a second. Nurse Gruery offered the tetanus shot and would have done the injection, but the Doctor grabbed the stick and roughly jabbed the patient with an emphatic sigh.

After applying antiseptic and a bandage, Nurse Gruery left the room thinking, "I've never seen the Doctor treat a patient that roughly. I'm glad I'm not a friend of hers."

Dr. Bramton sat down and filled out some paperwork. Joe put on his jacket as all his other clothes had been cut to pieces.

"Joe, I don't know what to do with you. Your wife calls me crying all the time about your exploits. First you flirt with the wrong women in a bar and get beaten within an inch of your life. You even broke three bones in your hand in that fight."

"Hitting that guy in the face was like punching a brick wall. But it was the only shot I got in."

"So, I help convince your wife that taking up fishing will keep you out of trouble and what happens? You have four serious accidents in eighteen months and in every case you wait hours to get treatment. Are you nuts?" She went on without letting him answer.

"First you decide that you want to cook some food before you go fishing, but being drunk, you over-pump the Coleman stove. Like a dumbass, you examined the spilled gas with a lit cigarette in your mouth, and caused an explosion. You burn or singe half your hair, one eyebrow, parts of your neck, and your shoulder. Worried about a destroyed picnic table in a public park, you run away by going fishing. You come for treatment thirteen hours later and ask if I can hide the red color of your burned skin."

"I didn't know that the pump only needed three shots, I thought you had to feel it get pressurized."

"Next you manage to impale your nipple with a musky lure with the fish still attached. That caused so much bruising that half your chest turned black and blue."

"I thought hand landing would be easy, Marv does it all the time. Once she gave a flip and hooked me, it was a circus trying to get her calmed down so Marv could cut that hook. She was released alive, though. I needed a money shot of a nice fish with my partner's hand-made lure in the fish's mouth. How was I to know she'd flip the front hooks into my shirt? I thought that that was all it was, my shirt, until Marv tried to reach in and cut the hook that was in me. That's when she flipped again and caught the cuff of the glove he was wearing with the middle hook. That fish really took a notion to start shaking then. It hurt a lot when she shook; with her on the last treble hook, Marv's arm on the middle hook, and me on the first. I was worried then that we'd never get loose and the three of us would have to come see you."

"If you ever bring a smelly dead fish in my clinic, I'll kill you!"

"Take it easy! Marv slipped his hand out of the glove with the hook in it. And after I yelled at him a little, he figured out to cut the hook in the fish instead of the one that I now knew was in my nipple. That pain, caused by the shaking and jumping, stopped after awhile. But, I guess it did bruise pretty bad."

"Yet you fished another three hours!"

"Well, it's a long way to Pantherville and we don't get many days off in the construction business. My chest did kind of stiffen up as the day wore on, though."

"Then you went for a second round with the Coleman stove and burned all the hair off your right hand and arm. I guess since that wasn't a serious burn, I can forgive that."

"I can't, that one was stupid. I think it was Musky Bill who said that fire on a boat is the worst danger, because the only way to put out the fire is to sink the boat. We figured, if we ate on the boat, we could keep fishing. But we made a mess and got onion smell all over the lures. Did you know muskies don't like the smell of onions, bananas, or oranges?"

"I don't care what muskies like! I want you to stop coming in here! I want you to not get hurt! I don't want to keep treating your mishaps!"

"All right, already, can I go home now? I gotta work tomorrow."

At the next meeting of the musky club, Joe had the eighty dollars for a landing net in his hand and was getting up to buy one from Tiny, the club treasurer, when Marv caught his arm and said, "I'll land the fish from now on, save your money." Joe bought another round of beers.

Chapter 2

June 6th

"I told you. I don't get along with these people," Joe Gaspe was whining. Marv was not used to that.

"Just tell me if I can turn this rig around without getting clipped! We're heading back to the US of A and thank God I'm not going to jail in Canada for you." Marv had lost patience with Joe. They'd been through two hours of waiting, numerous repetitions of the same questions, and snotty people speaking French in their presence and now were being sent back across the bridge. They'd been denied entry to Ontario and Marv hoped they could sail through US customs. Standing outside with his truck and boat trailer, Marv had been assaulted by the hot smells of a border entry station. Diesel exhaust, sticky asphalt, ill-tuned autos of every make and model emitting their characteristic odors that rolled over Marv in waves. He had been left outside most of the time while Joe was inside being ignored, questioned, and gossiped about. Briefly, Marv had been pulled inside, questioned, and made to wait in a room crammed with people speaking so many languages that his head started to pound.

Eventually, a Francophone agent told him to go outside and wait by his truck. "Not in ze truck, by ze truck." Joe was the guy they were worried about. Marv wondered, not for the first time, why he part-nered-up with Gaspe. Sure, they'd been friends since high school and they were involved financially with the boat and trailer and fishing gear, but Joe could be a real pain in the ass. He was always doing stupid stuff and attracting the attention of the authorities. But, anyway, they were on the way back to New York. Marv Ankara knew that Joe would rattle on about what happened in there all the way back to Muskedaigua.

A tractor-trailer emblazoned with French logos went by and Joe said, "Punch it now before that next truck." With tires squealing, engine roaring, Marv shouting, "Jesus, Joe, are you trying to get me killed?" The turn was as tight as the rig could make and the next semi blasted its air horn as they got into the lane going back to the states.

"Those people just don't like me. I've never been convicted of anything."

"Yeah Joe, that doesn't mean you've never done anything illegal, now does it?"

"No, it doesn't."

Marv Ankara and Joe Gaspe had met when Marv took a course, called wood shop in the old days, now known as technology. Joe had been taking shop for four years and had become the de-facto instructor with a special talent for airbrushed paint applications. Before high school in Muskedaigua, Joe's history was a closed book, sealed, buried, never spoken about.

"You're a Mohawk aren't you, eh?" A female Canadian Border Agent in full tactical gear, who was reading off a sheet of fax paper, had asked Joe. She couldn't keep the paper, from an older machine, from curling up because she was tiny and had the hands of a child. Joe noticed how big the Glock looked on her hip and idly wondered where they got such a miniscule uniform.

"My stepmother was Mohawk so technically I am of the people." Joe left out the fact that his Mother was also Mohawk.

"You were a radical AIM member, weren't you?"

"I am a carpenter in Muskedaigua, New York, where I've lived since I was two. A hard charging construction worker." Joe was doing that thing he did with his eyes. The thing that women had trouble resisting. He was not an attractive man: he had a large head, a mop of coarse hair, was missing a front tooth at the time, and his nose had been serially broken, causing it to wander across his face. But Joe had a self-deprecating smile and a twinkle in his eye and a way of saying naïve things that made women want to like him. He wasn't huge but gave the impression of being a lovable big lug. He was twinkling those eyes now, even though he was scared. He didn't want to end his days in Canada. He knew that they knew some stuff about him, but wondered if they knew everything. Heck, even he couldn't remember everything.

He saw the irony in his situation even if the parade of Canadian officials took his presence in their country as a national catastrophe. Officer Reynaud was back for her second go at Joe. She'd been the first to interview him when Marv's truck had been pulled over.

Officer Reynaud's initial questions were followed by several more from her supervisor, who spoke in rapid French, a language Joe barely recognized. The supervisor switched to accented English, asked questions about a 1990 arrest near a Mohawk reservation bonfire. Suddenly, he left the room.

Then came a member of the OPP (Ontario Provincial Police) who stressed his non-French ancestry and asked where he and Marv had been going. In spite of the obvious evidence, fishing boat, trailer, and tackle, the cops didn't believe the Ottawa River fishing trip story.

Then the Straits Regional Police representative had asked a lot of questions about who owned the boat, (Joe) where was the receipt, (he'd won the boat in a charity fundraiser) who owned the trailer, (Marv) was it registered, (yes) and where they were going, (again). This was another Francophone and he went out of his way to be snotty. Joe wondered whether they tried to be obnoxious, the way a football player tries to be tough.

Finally the RCMP sent in a fellow who was English, again. He asked if Joe had ever been (pronounced bean) to Detroit (pronounced de troy it), or was a member of a radical organization (pronounced with a stressed long I in the middle). The Mountie had abruptly left the room and conferred with a slight, dapper, black man in an office visible over the shoulder of the diminutive Officer Reynaud, who began interrogating Joe again.

"Fishing on the Ottawa River, eh? You say you won a charter trip, then why bring your own boat and motor?"

"We were going to learn the waters from the charter and then fish on our own for a few days. Apply the learning, that's what the musky fisherman does."

"You only had one hundred dollars each, how were you going to pay for accommodations, food, and fuel with that?"

"We sleep in the truck, eat little, and spend the money on gas."

"Are you aware that the locals don't look favorably on you doing that?"

"I am now."

"Are you aware that sleeping in a vehicle is vagrancy?"

"Then I'd be eligible for welfare, eh?"

In spite of herself, Officer Reynaud cracked a brief smile, "Deportation, more likely," she said.

"I'm sorry officer I wasn't aware that one couldn't sleep in a camper top in Ontario."

"Not on the roadside, only in a registered campsite, licensed by the municipality, province, and federal government and inspected by environment Canada."

"Don't want me taking a leak on the ground, eh?"

"It is illegal to urinate in the Province of Ontario." The officer failed to see the ridiculous nature of the last statement. Joe opened his mouth, thought, shut his mouth and waited for what was next.

A few minutes went by, Officer Reynaud shuffled papers, took notes, and finally looked toward the door to the adjoining office when the Mountie and the black gentleman entered. The Mountie gave a head nod to her and she left.

The Mountie said, "Joe Gaspe this is a representative of your nation." He turned on his heel and left.

Joe could see this probably wasn't a Mohawk, so the nation mentioned must be the United States.

"Thomas Andre, Assistant Special Agent in Charge, Federal Bureau of Investigation Pantherville Office" said the business card presented to Joe. This was the first person who had identified himself to Joe. The others were all stuffed uniforms. Agent Andre looked back toward the glass door. Both men heard an audible click and the people in the outer office disappeared through the several doors.

"Let's talk, Joe." The FBI man was short, quiet, well dressed, and superlatively groomed, obviously in command of the situation. Warily, Joe improved his posture and demeanor, remembering his Irish grandmother's admonition to, "Sit up straight and act like you've got some class."

The FBI man took the best part of an hour explaining to Joe that he was being offered an opportunity he would be unable to refuse. Joe made him repeat the whole offer before he asked any specific questions.

"You're aware that I've had an issue or two with the law, right? I was a bit of a scrapper in my youth, though I'm too slow for that now."

"Your possession of physical courage may come in handy in this endeavor." The FBI man knew a lot about him. Joe wondered how much.

"I've had some traffic issues and got caught with pot twice when I was younger, you know?"

Agent Andre nodded saying, "Criminal records and traffic records are easily reviewed."

Hoping that they might not know everything, Joe decided to try another tack.

"Why me? What do I have to give up? What's in it for me?" Joe asked.

"You are a man who can keep secrets. You can provide results without details. You make friends easily with all types of people. Besides a chance to help your country in a real tangible way, we are offering you a twenty-one-foot Boston Whaler with twin outboards—185 Mercury four strokes—in a slip on the musky straits, Royal Marina to be exact.

"In return we want you to form a network of informants—all quite unofficial—who will keep you abreast of suspicious happenings, then you will let me know where our agents should be and when they should be there. We want you to keep us up-to-date on the activities of certain parties before they create chaotic situations."

"How do I get the information?"

"Two ways: recruit people who are aware of what is happening on the Musky Straits in the course of their daily lives, and cultivate your friendship with Mel Dumke. He will lead you to the persons of interest. We don't want Dumke touched until he's provided us with the spade to dig up the dormant ones."

"How did you…?"

"We listen to a lot of chatter—the amount that is in English is easiest to monitor."

"How can I form a network?"

"You inform me of who you think could be helpful and unobtrusive and I will contact that person and determine his suitability and activate him, or not."

"How do you know you can trust me?"

"For what we want you to do, we are confident in you."

Joe liked this little guy but was also put off by how much the agent seemed to know of his affairs.

"Now, it's all right if I musky fish with this boat of yours, right?"

"We wish you would, the more you and your network are on the water, the better."

"Going back over this, just to see if I'm dreaming. You are going to smooth over my problems with the North, er Canada."

Agent Andre said, "Yes."

You're going to restore my driver's license."

"Yes, though that will take six months. State officials sometimes feel the need to impress the Federal government"

"How do I get around, on land I mean?"

"You will be provided with a driver, an intern actually."

Joe laughed at that, "An intern? Heh, heh, heh."

"You're going to give me a boat, a Boston Whaler with twin 185 Mercs at that."

"Yes."

"You're going to rent, for me, a boathouse to moor my new boat at Royal Marine."

"Yes."

"You're going to pay me $5000.00 per month, plus expenses, create a story for my wife that I'm on a long term construction project in Pantherville, and all you want me to do is go musky fishing a lot, create a network of observers of the local border scene, and warn you if I hear of anything."

"That's about it." Agent Thomas Andre paused and looked at the beaming smile on Gaspe's face. Then he summarized his position. "I approached you on this matter, not as a representative of the Bureau, though I am that, but as a representative of the overall Department of Homeland Security.

"All the agencies of the Department are supposed to be cooperating now, but in reality, all that means is that the higher-ups meet for lunch once in a while. On the operational level we have no way of communicating—have no structure—and have no way of cooperating. Besides, with multiple agencies, thousand of employees and politics being as bitter as they are, there are hundreds of potential, and actual, leakers. We know that some or all of our agencies have been penetrated by agents of Al Qaida, and that we can't do much about it in any reasonable time frame. We also know your good buddy, Mel Dumke," Andre held up his hand to stop Joe's interruption. "Mel Dumke works for several bad actors, but he is our way in to these networks. Through you."

"Mel is just a guy I bought some musky gear from when he quit musky fishing. When I call a guy my good buddy—he's an ass."

"Nevertheless, you and Mel have suffered similar setbacks in your career development. It should be easy to convince him of something he wishes to believe. That all persons so affected are bitter, vengeful, and driven by 'resentiment'."

"That's French, hey, resentiment?"

"Yes, Joe, it is French."

"So what is Dumke into, smuggling illegals? Smuggling drugs?

Smuggling weapons? Terrorism? Smuggling weapons of mass destruction, poisons, and nukes?"

"Yes."

"That bastard. All that stuff, huh?"

"And murder. I must warn you, we think that Mel Dumke has arranged the murder of an agent of ours and we are presently trying to extricate another Chinese-American of ours who is compromised. This is a dangerous assignment, Joe. Will you do it?"

"Clean slate with the Canucks, even that dust-up in 1990 forgotten, clean driving record, boat on the Musky Straits with boathouse, five grand a month, my wife content. What's not to like? Count me in. Oh yeah, and a long shot at revenge for 9/11."

"Remember, Joe, what we want is a heads-up for a potential problem, we don't want details of how you found out and we don't want Dumke served up on a silver platter. He's our entree into the shadow world. This is war, Joe, and everything is fair in war—as long as the *New York Times* doesn't know about it."

"OK, great, how do I contact you?"

"You and Marv go down to Royal Marine and see Brad, he'll set you up with the boat and boathouse. Fish for the weekend just like you'd planned, only do it around Pantherville. On Sunday night, as you head home, stop at the payphone at Straits Avenue and Myrtle and call this number." He handed Joe a sticky note. "You'll be informed of what to do next."

"Wow, OK." Joe Gaspe left the customs office and joined Marv.

"That was the toughest interview of my life," Joe told Marv.

Afraid to ask for details, Marv had started the truck to head back into the good old US of A.

Jackie Bertwilliger was counting worms on a fine June morning. He filled a Styrofoam cup with one dozen and put it in a stack then filled a larger cup with two dozen and put it in another stack. Bait, like doughnuts and eggs, was sold in dozens through long-standing practice. He'd wondered why a time or two but never tried selling night crawlers in tens and twenties.

Not every customer in a bait store is going fishing immediately after their purchase; some people are getting bait between other errands. Few however came into Jackie's Big Haul bait shop as well-dressed as the black guy who'd just walked through the door. He was wearing a conservative, high-quality tailored, charcoal gray suit and he wore it well. Pride in appearance was obvious in his manner, though he revealed no squeamishness as he walked up to the big tub of mucky black soil from which Jackie was removing handfuls of squirming crawlers and counting them quietly to himself, moving his lips slightly.

Jackie had noticed the man enter his store and noticed that he walked past the line of three customers in front of his assistant. He'd been expecting this visit ever since his long chat with Joe Gaspe.

"Hello, Mr. Bertwilliger, I'm Thomas Andre. Can we talk somewhere?"

"Sure. Just a sec." Jackie squeezed a few ribbons of muck back into the large container, stacked his most recent small container, and turned to the sink behind him to wash his hands. "Got to cover this tight or the pesky crawlers will escape. They're fast as hell." Jackie secured the lid on the plastic container and said, "Let's go through here."

They moved through a door that had a sign on it reading, "Private! Entrance by prior arrangement only." They were in the private bar room section of Jackie's business. There was no one in the room and only one recessed light was lit. Jackie ushered Mr. Andre to a round table and they sat facing each other at an angle.

Thomas Andre presented a business card that identified him as working for the Department of Homeland Security. "Special Projects" was the only other identifier—no phone number, fax, cell, or address was listed. "I assume by your manner that Joe Gaspe has told you to expect me."

"Yeah, we had quite the chat. It took me a while to believe that my wild man cousin was working on this project" (Jackie pronounced it PRO ject) "but I guess you're the proof of the pudding, eh?" When he was nervous, Jackie B's Canadian idioms came through sometimes, despite his being a US citizen for twenty years.

"I have been called many things in my life that may be a first time for that one. I won't go into the rationale for choosing Joe, stepson of your uncle Frank, but it is his special access as a man of the edges and shadows that has qualified him for this ongoing project. He has been establishing contact with people who have business reasons or other reasons to be along the waterfront area, especially those who are there at non-peak hours and seasons. I assume that your workers and those free-lancers with whom you speak are observant." This last word was left hanging in the air as a question and an invitation to comment.

"Bait dealers and brokers gossip the way old washerwomen do. I hear about everything, unusual or not. But, as I told Joe, I can listen more closely from now on."

"That will be fine. You are aware that we wish you to take no action on your own; just observe and call the number on that card," Jackie turned it over and saw a handwritten phone number on the back. "Any time day or night, or you can just tell Joe Gaspe. We want to know about unusual activity and we want to know about any plans you might hear of. Are you familiar with a gentleman named Mel Dumke?"

"Old flat-headed Mel? Sure, I know him."

"He is a person of interest who we feel will lead us to some very bad characters. It is especially important that you do not let on to him that fact, but encourage his bragging when he is under the influence. To remove Mr. Dumke from the equation would be counterproductive, right now. You and Joe are the only people I have told this to. I know that Mr. Dumke frequents this establishment and I hope that you will make him welcome."

"OK. If that will help, I'll do it."

"Do you have any questions for me?"

"Who else is in this network of Joe's?"

"It is very eclectic as only Joe Gaspe could make it. Only Joe and I know the exact makeup of the network, who is in it. It is wide and deep and not confined to the waterfront."

"You're looking for information about terrorism, drugs, illegal aliens, what?"

"All those and anything else worrisome, chemicals, fuel, shipping, if it bothers you or seems out of place, let us know."

"I've got it. You can consider me on the job right now."

"I thank you, sir, and your country thanks you as well." Agent Thomas Andre left by the side screen door, the private side of Jackie B's.

Chapter 3

June 17th

"I think this guy is from the desert," said Joe Gaspe, whose ethnic identity comments were getting to Radleigh Loonch. She'd been assigned to shadow Gaspe by her boss. It was her first non-training assignment as a probationary intern for the U.S. Customs and Border Patrol Agency. Rad didn't yet understand what she was supposed to keep an eye on or report about. She had been running with Gaspe for three days and hadn't said too much. It was hard for her to figure out whether she was supposed to be aloof from Gaspe, gain his confidence, note his every misstep, or go with the flow and try keeping him from a big blunder.

She'd gotten the job with the CBP department because she spoke and read Spanish better than many natural Spanish speakers. She was sure she'd end up on the Mexican border, but instead she'd reported to Hubert Hilliard in the Pantherville office. After a two-week orientation, she'd been designated for the assignment of being sidekick to Joe Gaspe. Gaspe wasn't a government employee but a free-lance subcontractor who seemed to work for everyone and no one.

Rad had already met Gerhard Blog, Gaspe's shadow from the U.S. Army Corps of Engineers and Kyle Buchhalter doing the same job for the U.S. Coast Guard. Rad deduced that the newfound requirement for cooperation to all these disparate agencies had to do with the powers assigned to the director of the Department of Homeland Security. But, "Nobody was telling her nothing." Rad had a nagging feeling that the cooperation among agencies was a lot like spying on each other. So, mostly she listened and tried not to let her facial expressions or body language give out any clues.

When she'd been pulled from training early and brought into the room with Mr. Hilliard there'd been a slight, unnamed, sharply dressed gentleman of African-American descent in the room observing the interview. He had said nothing then, but here he was on the dais for the Multi-Agency Regional Steering Committee for Awareness and Responsibility in Case of Imminent National Emergencies (M.A.R.S.C.A.R.I.N.E.), Section X Region GL for the USA and Canada. Various agencies were represented, in the persons of their most important local officials and staff, at this meeting. Each official emphasized his importance by the number of staff, aides, and retainers he brought to the meeting. There were the FBI, the Border Patrol, the Coast Guard, the Army Corps of Engineers, the Pantherville City Police, the Musky County Sheriff, and from Canada, the RCMP, the OPP, and the Cascades Parks Police and the Cascades Regional Police Service. The Canadians looked exquisitely bored with the proceedings while eagerly waiting for the bar to be opened at the next break.

Shlomo Antontrowicz, of the US Army Corps, had been lisping his way through a presentation to one of his employees when he had been the target of the desert comment from Gaspe. Rad tried to listen and suppress the slow burn that Joe's anti-Semitic comment raised in her.

Shlomo said, "It was Dale's idea to stop the infiltration of illegal immigrant individuals in the shadow compartments of trains by x-raying the false ends of the gondola cars as they passed by the inspection stations. This has been a ringing success, as we have nabbed four stowaways in the first four days. In honor of this innovation I hereby present Dale Newfy with the engineer of the year award." There was polite applause as Shlomo finished his speech, posed for photos, and took his seat.

The Moderator, Thomas Andre, Assistant Special Agent in Charge of the Pantherville office of the FBI, called for a fifteen minute break before the final speakers of the afternoon.

"I'm going to hit the pisser," said Joe. Unable to follow, Rad noticed Ger Blog, whose gaze never seemed to leave Gaspe, head into the men's room right behind him. Radleigh now realized that the silent man in her interviews with Hilliard had been an important man in the FBI office. She couldn't figure out why a little old probationary employee with a Spanish minor had drawn the attention of the higher-ups in two federal agencies. Rad made her way to the bar where the Canadian delegation was crowding the beer tap. She needed a Diet Coke and a chance to think about her assignment.

An unobtrusive Asian man sat at the Army Engineer's table with his mind engaged elsewhere. Sam Hung was thinking about his mother and whether the takeover of Hong Kong by the mainland Chinese would give him an opening to get her out of there and into the United States or Canada. This thought consumed him in his private moments. Publicly, at venues like this meeting, he was a hale fellow, swapping nerdy stories with other engineers. He'd given himself the nickname "Lucky" even though Sam, an anglicized pronunciation of Sung, was itself a nickname.

While the engineers argued over who had the heaviest bag of snack-sized potato chips—the minute variations in these items were fascinating to them—Sam's mind was on the dilemma he found himself in. It was a dilemma that had no real solution, only a continuing commitment. He was a trapped man.

Rad remembered the uncomfortable interview with her boss.

"I need you to stay with Gaspe as much as you can," said Mr. Hilliard. "He's a loose cannon on deck, we are afraid of his methods, and worry that our prosecutions of anyone he leads us to will not be good. So, if he helps us avert disasters while the court cases are less than satisfactory, he will merely be another complication in an already complicated world."

"What am I supposed to do about his actions?"

"We need advanced warning, not at the last possible second, so we can take over deterrence and apprehension of alleged suspects." Hilliard had said. The slight dapper black man sat quietly, looking at his fingernails when Radleigh looked at him. She suspected he looked at her when she was not looking at him.

"So, I'm to slip away and call you when I suspect or discern something is going down?"

"We'll be giving you a prepaid cell phone that dials a twenty four-seven operator who will listen for you to name time and place and a short description of details. The operator will relay the information to the appropriate parties."

"Is Joe supposed to know I'm doing this?"

"We'd prefer he didn't. Joe is no danger to you—he's not going to harm you—he's a danger to himself and all humanity with his occasional reckless behavior, however."

"If he's such a wild man, why not cut him loose?"

Hilliard looked at some papers on his desk, shifted his eyes to the man who would eventually be revealed as Assistant Special Agent in Charge Thomas Andre—Rad thought she saw a barely perceptible nod—and brought his gaze back to Rad. "What I'm going to say next is for your ears only. If you claim I said it, I will deny it, do you understand?"

Rad nodded tentatively.

"Since 9/11 there are things that we need to know, and things we need to do, that are extralegal—no agent or officer or supervisors can know about them. A person like Joe Gaspe who travels in a world of shadows and edges and knows people of many types gives us access to information—information that, even if we found it, we would be too late to act on. Information that can never be confirmed as fact—legally—but which we know to be true; information that if they knew we knew, our sources would dry up and blow away. Information that is vital to the security of our country and the safety and protection of this border crossing. This border crossing with our four bridges and miles of shoreline is very vulnerable and susceptible to attack. Gaspe can penetrate this netherworld without our enemies knowing he's done it and sometimes he doesn't know he's done it."

Radleigh Loonch was taking this all in but not really digesting the enormity of her new job. She was an attractive, tall, and bright college-educated woman, whose anthropology degree qualified her to work at few jobs in the world. Her father had encouraged her to apply at the U. S. Customs and Border Patrol Agency (CBP). Since the creation of the Department of Homeland Security, CBP was hiring college grads aggressively. Rad had been profiled for serious assignment quickly by her supervisors. She was self-confident, assertive, and skeptical. Though she had an attractive round face, framed by well-groomed brown hair, her doubtful, stoic expression made it obvious to an observer that she would be nobody's fool.

"You will be interviewed each Friday evening when Joe goes with his wife for his habitual fish fry. The agent speaking with you will know what questions to ask and give you a rough agenda of the things to look for in the week ahead." Hilliard paused to let this sink in.

"Gaspe knows who you work for and has his own ideas of what you are doing. He is also going to be observed by an intern from the US Army Corps of Engineers—they are in charge of all non-private facilities on the US/Canada border—and the US Coast Guard which has an obvious interest in the waterway. You'll meet those interns and their controllers later today. Gaspe is such a prime source that he in fact works for all three of those US Government entities."

Rad was beyond the point of asking questions. She couldn't imagine where to start.

After Ms. Loonch left his office, Hilliard turned to Andre, a man of whom he was unsure. Since they came from different agencies within Homeland Security, were they obliged to recognize relative rank? What were equivalent ranks in CBP and FBI? Did the importance of their agencies within the super bureaucracy matter? Hilliard was unsure about all of this.

"Are you sure about this Joe Gaspe character? He sounds like a screw-up to me."

"There's been hard times in the rust belt for decades. Not everyone who"s been slammed by the economy is a screw-up."

"Still, are you confident of his loyalties?"

"Joe is loyal to the US if that is what you are asking. I am dead-on certain sure of that. My father told me, and this is the most important thing he ever said, 'It doesn't matter what cards are in the hand dealt to you, all that matters is how you play the hand.' Joe has reacted to his setbacks by getting up and going back to work or working harder. He's never lost his faith in the US or the American way. He knows Dumke and Dumke knows him. Besides, if Dumke sees him as a fellow screw-up, a sympathetic character, well, that's all the better."

"If you think Dumke drove the van that transported your agent, Chang's, body why don't you arrest him?" Hilliard was unconvinced about Joe Gaspe, though he was out of his sphere of influence.

"It is thought by those that matter, that Dumke will lead us to places we cannot get close to without him. He will remain at large at this time." Thomas Andre could resort to bureaucratic doublespeak at any time.

"Is he CIA? Are you reluctant to tread on their turf?" This was an uncharacteristically direct question for Hubert Hilliard.

"The Central Intelligence Agency is tasked with foreign intelligence. Their agents work outside of US borders." Andre's non-answer ended the conversation.

Rad was jolted from her thoughts by a question.

"Whaddya say we blow this pop stand before the really boring speeches begin?" It was Joe Gaspe, at her elbow, with Ger Blog looming not far behind. Rad was startled by Joe's stealthy approach and noticed that she hadn't touched her Diet Coke, though everyone was filing back to his seat.

"It's only going to be the Canadians talking and they haven't liked me since my younger days. My father left Canada for Muskedaigua and they've been pissed at the Gaspes ever since." Joe broke into his signature laugh at this point, a laugh like a machine gun directed at anyone but, most often at himself. Joe had a way of projecting a "big dummy" image that communicated to the listener that he wasn't really dumb at all.

"Come on, let's cut a trail." Rad took a big slug of her soft drink and followed Gaspe out the side door leaving behind her seminar materials and obeying her prime directive, to shadow Joe Gaspe.

Radleigh turned to see that Agent Andre had noticed. Walking behind Gaspe she remarked to herself on the size of his big shaggy head, the stoutness of his body, and the unkempt look of his person. There was no detail about Joe Gaspe that was appealing, but the total affect of him was that of a comfortable couch, broken in, rather than past its prime. Rad was an unusual woman in a lot of ways, but like many women she found something appealing in a man who was a little bit dangerous and not too pretty.

Joe Gaspe, though he talked like a bigot, (I hate everybody," he'd said), acted the fool, told corny jokes, and thought himself to be something special, had an appealing quality. He was genuine and uniquely American.

It was a source of concern for Radleigh Loonch coming from the world of academia, where political correctness had overrun the farm, to hear the use of ethnic descriptors and slurs liberally sprinkled throughout the casual speech of so many people on the open range of the work world. Of course, she reasoned these were mechanics and bait dealers and construction workers. They were polite. They were willing to take people as they were. But they were composed of all rough edges, without polish or finish to themselves. Somehow, though, she liked most of them for their lack of pretension and for their practical charm.

Rad had broken with her Ivy League orientation in her junior year in college, when she developed a taste for country music, not in spite of the simplicity of its themes but because of the simplicity that recommended itself to the real spirit and fact of America. It had no pretense to being Euro or sophisticated but reveled in its earthy down-home style. The rough and tumble appeal of country music was precisely the appeal of Joe Gaspe

"I love a magnolia tree in June, but I don't even know what they look like after the blossoms fall, never had one in my yard, I guess." Rad was driving down Straits Avenue when Joe Gaspe surprised her with this. It was now mid-June and he waved at a tree-filled yard on his side of the street.

"Joe, you need to stop with the ethnic slurs around me. I don't like it. Don't want to hear it and you tick me off when you do it. I want to like you. I do like you. But you need to be better about this racist stuff."

"Aren't you the touchy one? Okay, okay, don't give me that look. My mother was a Mohawk, my stepmother, who raised me was a Mohawk. We see all of you, whites, blacks and yellows, as invaders and consider your differences—your ethnicity—as meaningless. Besides, I'm a Heinz 57 myself. I've got everything in me. My step-dad was a French Canadian carpenter in Muskedaigua. My real father was an Irishman whose father was a Jewish trader. An Irish Jew, ain't that a hoot? Changed his name from Sol Mitzel to Arthur McGinley. I've got a grandmother who is a full blooded Gypsy."

"That's Roma, Joe, not Gypsy." Rad's anthropology degree came with some language restrictions.

"Roma's a tomato, grandma was a gypsy. If you ever saw her you'd know. My mother's father was an Italian of Austrian lineage, tall, blond, and sturdy like a tree. His wife, my other grandmother, was the Mohawk Clan Mother, Lucyaneda, who traced part of her ancestry back to Louis Cook. Do you know who Louis Cook was?" Joe didn't wait for Rad's answer.

"He was a black boy captured by the Mohawks near Saratoga, adopted into the tribe—the Mohawks adopted any captives that appealed to them in order to replace fallen members of their clans. My grandmother's great-great grandfather was Louis Cook, who was awarded a medal by George Washington for service in the Revolutionary war. With regard to ethnicity, I am everything and nothing, because being a Mohawk is a way of living and dreaming, not a race. But I like you, Rad, so I'll go easy on you with the comments."

Rad was driving her Malibu and Joe was giving her directions,

"Left here, right at the next stop sign, left again at the light."

This aggravated Rad, who asked, "Where are we going? I can find anything around here on my own." Of course, Joe knew of her German need for "ordnung" and that's why he gave her directions in such an obnoxious way. Joe knew how to create tension when it suited his purpose.

"Stop! Back up! Turn in here and park."

They were in the back parking area of an apartment building with several shabby vehicles at odd angles. Joe got out and started walking.

"Aren't you going to lock your door?"

"I never lock a car. That just invites thieves to break windows."

"Joe! You don't have a car. This is my car, lock the door, you loser."

"Go ahead," Joe said over his shoulder as he walked away.

They went through the parking lot, down a driveway, into another lot filled with SUVs and pickup trucks. They came in a side door with a piece of notebook paper taped to it that read "Jackie B's Draft Beer and Live Bait." Rad had been here before to buy bait when fishing with her dad, but she'd come in the front door where the sign read "Big Haul Live Bait."

Jackie B's place, an ordinary bait and tackle shop, had a neon sign in one window that said "Live Bait" and a bumper sticker glued on the outside of the window that said, "Muskies: All Other Fish Are Just Bait." This was where the local community of musky fishermen hung out and where Joe made a lot of his contacts.

"A beaver hates the sound of rushing water and will work continuously to put a stop to it. Anyone who knows nature would know that. It didn't have to be one of the people of the Six Nations."

Radleigh Loonch heard this statement as she and Gaspe approached a round table, occupied by a man who looked like an archetype of a Mohawk Indian. He was talking to two other fisher-men, one of whom was her Uncle Rudyard. The man with the Mohawk hair-do had made the statement while inclining his head toward another man in the bar. That one, with a head as flat as a Kansas wheat field, was just going out the screen door.

Rad sat next to Joe in the chair he motioned towards. "Mo, this is my shadow, Radleigh Loonch. Rad, my Indian cousin, Moses X Snow, known to everyone as Mo Snow. He imports worms from Canada."

"From the Mohawk Nation," he corrected as he bathed Rad with a disarming smile. "My cousin Joe likes to call us Indians even though he is one of us, a member of the Six Nations." Mo clapped Gaspe on his shoulder and mimicked an offended glare.

Rad was getting used to the easy manner in which Joe Gaspe and his friends commented about ethnicity, but she didn't approve.

They were in the special friends area of Jackie B's. It was a room next door to the bait and tackle shop that had once been a bar & grill. Now it was a meeting room where fishermen and hunters could pay $2 and draw all the beer they wanted from the keg of Molson's Canadian behind the bar. There was no wine, liquor, or soda pop: it was beer or nothing. Non-drinkers could bring a bottle of Diet Coke through from the machine in the bait shop. Rad wasn't against beer drinking, but had found it necessary to start well after Joe Gaspe, if she was to keep her wits as he slaked his mighty thirst. Joe didn't drink all the time but drank seriously when he did and always seemed to do his fact-finding better when the beer flowed.

"Who was that guy?" Rad asked pointing a finger at the screen door.

"That was my old buddy, Mel Dumke." Gaspe's references to people were opaque; everyone who wasn't his old buddy was his cousin or his partner or a good man. He came from a robust line of progenitors. He had six brothers and each of his parents had eleven siblings, so the cousins were legion. He also had seven businesses or hobbies, each with at least one partner.

"Dumke was telling us about the Oriental guy the state cops just dug out of a beaver dam on the Rez." said Mo Snow.

"Some kids were giggin' frogs when their old hound started digging in the beaver dam upstream and they found this Oriental guy," Joe added. He was informed about this too.

"People are Asian, Joe, rugs are Oriental," Rad corrected.

"Yeah, right, this Asian guy had been dumped there with his head bashed in and the killer knocked out a section of dam and counted on the beavers to bury the body. Which they'd done a fair job of, but I guess there is no place on the territory that is too remote for a pair of ten-year-old boys and a dog."

"Your old buddy Mel, seemed to know a lot about that. He's not one of us. Is he law enforcement?" Mo asked.

"Mel Dumke hates cops, all cops and all government employees, and all lawyers, preachers, and especially all musky fishermen. I don't know where he gets his news, but he does seem to have a lot of it. He's a bitter SOB."

"What have you white people got to be bitter about? Nobody stole your land or desecrated your sacred ground." Mo's eyes bored into Joe.

"Hey, I'm your cousin remember? Anyway, Mel got downsized by Bethlehem Steel, got fired at Trico, got arrested while working for Allied Chemical, and lost his Charter Captain's License when he was turned in for poaching muskies. He's had a rough stretch, then he got arrested for beating up his girlfriend and accused of molesting her daughter. He's got reasons to be bitter." Gaspe looked askance at Rad, letting on he didn't really sympathize with Mel Dumke.

"Wait a minute, you were laid off at Xerox, let go at Kodak, fired from your job with Crimini builders, and you've had run-ins with the law; you don't go around hating the world." Mo found Americans amusing and confusing.

"Different strokes for different folks, I don't dwell on the past unless it affects the present. I've never been convicted of anything, except one DUI and I was driving myself to a clinic that time. I'd just gotten the snot kicked out of me."

Joe went to the bar and filled two schooners from the tap. Schooners were twenty-two ounce mugs that Jackie B had picked up when the Schooner House fixtures were auctioned off.

Rad studied these cousins. She noted their differences as well as their similarities. Both had dark skin, though Joe was more olive and Mo more brick red, both had big heads, broad shoulders, and were stout and powerful looking. Mo Snow was over six feet tall, had the long torso, narrow hips, and strong legs typical of the Mohawks, while Joe was heavy all the way down. He had an offensive lineman's body with a big butt and heavy legs that came from a diet rich in chicken wings, pizza, hamburgers, and a lot of everything. Joe took equal pride in his appetite and his thirst.

Mo took hold of his Schooner like a lion taking down an antelope and drained it off in one long draught. Rad's thoughts were about life imitating art, imitating life, and imitating itself. At a glance, this was what seemed to be the case with Moses X. Snow. He had a Mohawk haircut designed along the lines of what Hollywood thought such a cut should be, modified by what rock musicians thought would make them look unique, stylized by an apparent desire to be authentic. Rad, the anthropologist, knew that the Mohawk hairdo, as modeled for early painters, was more like a cross between a brush cut and a top knot than a line of longish hair down the middle of the skull. The Keepers of The Eastern Door of the Six Nations were a warlike tribe who had conquered their way to glory with stone tipped arrows, spears, and war clubs. It was common in battle to take a scalp from a stunned or wounded adversary and move on. By wearing their hair as they did, the Mohawks were difficult to scalp and their hair made a poor trophy. Mo's hairdo impressed the uninformed and showed off his pride, despite its inauthentic reality.

"I like beer too much to drink a lot of it," Mo said as he rose from the table, nodded to Radleigh and said. "Ma'am."

"I'll get those Dento rods now, so I can head for the territory." Mo Snow was getting ready to leave. Joe rose also and went through the bar and back into the bait shop.

"Nice meeting you." Rad spoke to the Mohawk's back, but at the door he turned and smiled a broad smile and left an exaggerated wink with her.

Rad sat with her uncle and Ian Drakulitch, politely listening as Ian droned on about a project he was involved in. Ian had a part time consulting business as a boat broker. His was a safe business model as he never took possession of any boats and therefore had no monetary outlay at risk. Drakulitch would interview his customers thoroughly to determine their needs in a boat, then he would scour the newspapers, swap sheets, and marina websites in a three state area to find boats that would be worth inspecting. For his work he would charge an hourly rate of $50 and could only sustain his business through favorable word of mouth, which he received.

"I don't know what it is with Dumke, he doesn't seem to care how good the boats are that he's buying, two boats mind you, and he hasn't given me a maximum price yet." Ian, known as the cheapest man in the town of Clarissa, couldn't get his mind around the concept of people with needs not constrained by finances.

"Mel Dumke was down and out last I heard, perhaps he is purchasing these two boats as an intermediary," Rudyard said.

"Loonch, you have a grasp of the obvious. The thing is he doesn't care about getting a good boat, doesn't really need my services, and shows a preference for Coastliners, the worst boat out there."

"Dumke is hard to fathom." Rudi Loonch seemed bored with Ian and grunted in satisfaction as Drakulitch made his excuses and left Jackie B's. Loonch patted his book on the table beside him and smiled at his niece. She knew that he looked forward to the opportunity to get back into his book when everyone at the table moved on to their other tasks.

"What are you reading now, Uncle Rudi?"

Rudyard turned the cover around to face her and pushed the book slightly in her direction.

"*The Fireship*" by C. Northcote Parkinson." Joe Gaspe read this over Rad's shoulder as he returned to the table. "You read the strangest stuff there, partner."

"That is the Parkinson famous for Parkinson's Law, 'Work will expand to consume the time available to complete it.'"

"What's a Fireship?" Joe asked. Then he said to Rad, "I need to get something out of your Malibu, can I have the keys?" Rad handed Joe the keys.

"In old naval battles with wooden ships, a Fireship was grappled to enemy ships or works to cause fires and destruction, often to break through a blocking position." Rudyard Loonch was ever the teacher.

"I knew that." Joe said, with his signature laugh.

"Do you know the alternate meaning of Fireship?"

"No, but I'll bet you're going to tell me."

Glancing at his niece, giving a shrug and a sigh, Rudi explained, "Sailors, who had visited ladies of the night in port towns, called one who gave them what we would call today a sexually transmitted disease, a Fireship, due to the burning sensations experienced after the men returned to the sea."

Joe laughed, "I get it, a poxy doxy, eh?" Joe laughed again, took the keys, and went back out to deal with Moses Snow.

"Is that true?" Rad was acquainted with her Uncle's propensity to treat theories of his as established truths.

"Do you doubt me, child?" he asked with an arched brow.

Rad and her Uncle didn't sit alone for long; Jackie Bertwilliger, owner of the bait shop, joined them at the table. He was another of Joe's cousins. Rad had met him earlier when she spent a long time looking over the lures and rigs in the store. As a young girl, she had loved to accompany her dad when he went to hardware stores and bait shops. He invariably got in long discussions with the proprietors or other customers while she was left to look over, handle, and re-sort the items at her level. These things were sorted by size and type in bins and on hooks. Rad enjoyed imagining the uses and history of the items she examined. She always felt a sense of satisfaction organizing things in her mind while examining them in a catalog or in a store. She put it down to that sense of order so often found in those of German descent.

"Where's Dento?" Jackie B had come from the rest room and missed Joe going out of the shop. He referred to Joe by the name of his custom made musky rod, the Dr. Dento.

"He went to transfer some rods to Mr. Snow." Rad was being helpful.

"Mr. Snow? You mean that crazy Indian?"

"Native American," corrected Rad.

"Yeah, well when he comes back, give him this paperwork, there's a new order, a check for the Dentoes I've sold in the last month, and another note. Make sure he sees the note." This was said with Jackie giving the folded note three shakes before he walked away.

"Don't you want to give that to Joe yourself?" She pointed at the papers.

"Can't you be trusted? We work on the honor system around here."

"Of course I can be trusted."

"It was nice to deal with such an honest person," Jackie said as he gathered a pair of waders and some other equipment from hooks on the wall and reversed course and headed out the screen door.

"Nice to meet you, too."

Chapter 4

June 18th

"Do you like this Malibu? I hear that new cooling system is a mess."

"Yeah, I like it. It suits me. But I may trade up to an Impala now that I'm employed full time." Radleigh was driving south on route 16 through the moribund little towns of the western part of the state.

"Another Chevy, huh? You don't like foreign cars. You know, their quality is better. So they say." Joe always was probing, Rad wondered if he was probing for weakness.

"My father liked US cars. Always said they had more room for Americans, biscuit-eaters he called us, but I suspect he secretly thought he was supporting the US economy."

"A good man, your Dad. Did you know that he and I were partners? He is always stirring up issues in the musky club. Nobody knows how to take him, me included."

Radleigh Loonch wasn't surprised by her Dad's reputation. She often felt she also had that self-destructive gene that caused the Loonches to bite the hand that pats them.

"Joe, tell me about your cousin Mr. Snow."

"Mr. Snow? He'd like that. Just call him Mo. What do you want to know about him?"

"I don't know, he just seemed interesting. Not the kind of man you meet every day."

"Mo is full-blooded Mohawk. He's lived at Kahnawake or Akwesasne all his life. He was quite the athlete in his twenties: played lacrosse, hockey, football—Canadian football that is—and the thing he was best at was baseball. He was a fireballing relief pitcher in the late eighties on his way up in the majors, He had a ninety-plus mile-per-hour fastball. That didn't last, though."

"What happened?"

"His wife died in a car wreck. He was out in San Diego just after his call up with the big league team —they called him Big Injun, said he threw smoke."

Rad made a sound with her lips that sounded like tsk-tsk when she heard the politically incorrect nickname.

"After his wife died, that dust-up at Oka started between the Mohawks and the Frenchie police. That's where I met him. He's my cousin but we'd never met. He helped me out big time. Anyway, he never went back to baseball. He said he was a northern man, didn't like the heat in San Diego. Something in him died when his wife was killed."

"He's a businessman?"

"Sure, he's done a lot of things. Right now he runs a bait business. He's a big man on the Rez. As big a man as you can be without running a casino."

"He seems nice."

Joe looked at her out of the side of his eye, thinking how he'd never have said nice to describe Mo. Intimidating, fierce, impressive, maybe, but nice? He didn't think so.

They had just entered Delano, among the saddest of the sad towns on the way south to the Oil Seep Seneca Indian Reservation. Small towns, like Delano, had once had something going on, but it was hard to determine, now, what it had been. The west side of Route

16, which comprised the principle block of Main Street, was taken up by several churches. There was a sturdy Baptist Church and a New Age Bible Church in an old storefront. REED BUILDING ESTAB- LISHED 1865 said the sign at the peak of this tallest building in town.

The first floor of the Reed building had once been King's Hardware. That sign had faded out in the middle and was only read- able at the edges. The hardware store had been replaced by a Red & White grocery with a round logo. It was also faded and worn, cover- ing the center of the storefront above the windows. The building was one of those old grocery stores with twelve-foot ceilings wherein the clerk had needed a ladder to reach the top shelves in order to help the customers. As a church, the front window featured a huge sign saying "Pornography Ruins Families, Give it Up for the Lord." The shabbi- ness of the building spoke sadly about modern times wherein painting was too expensive even to be taken up by teenage boys.

The next building along Main street was an old department store now gone over to used books: "Romances, mysteries, Christian Books —open Wednesday 12–6 PM," read a sign that looked as if a five year old had lettered it. The slant of the "n" was reversed. The last building on the west side of Main Street was the Roman Catholic Church, more prosperous than the other two, but too new to be ornate.

The stores on the east side of the street were as shabby as an old man wearing a worn-out suit, shiny at the knees and elbows, baggy in the rear, and, as a final indignity, the man himself had begun to with- er away, leaving the unutterable sadness of an entity with almost everything gone. It was a husk containing a withered seed, beyond the rescue of any amount of nutrition, water, and fertilizer.

The buildings on this shabbier east side of Main, two bars, a tat- too parlor, and a dirty bookstore, had false fronts, each at least one story taller than the building's actual construction. It looked like a set in a western.

There was a bar called Scotchies, a pornography shop that announced itself with a sign that read "XXXXX DVDs, books, videos, off street parking, entrance in rear." That one made Joe laugh and laugh again. The porn store was flanked by another bar, called Sleepies. The last building was a former Bait and Tackle store gone over to a Tattoo Parlor. It had darkened windows and a security door. As Rad cruised through town observing the 30 mph speed limit, Joe shouted, "Pull over, I gotta go in there!" He bailed out of the car while it was still rolling to a stop and ran across the street. Before Rad could ask what he was doing, he'd gone into the tattoo parlor.

The only building on either side which showed any but the barest minimum of maintenance was the town hall—a white painted building in the federal style, well landscaped—bustling because, as the sign said, "Traffic court today."

People hung on in these dying towns by driving fifty or one hundred miles to work every day. Twenty percent were on public assistance, fifty percent were old without any prospect of moving to a warmer climate, ten percent provided services for the local residents, ten percent worked locally, and ten percent made the drive to Pantherville or its suburbs to work. Pantherville, shabby and fading in its own right, still was the nexus of well-paying jobs in the area.

Slightly to the north of the sleazy east side of Main there was a small strip plaza that held the bank, post office, drug store, and convenience store. A Melnick's Roofing Company truck sat in the parking lot with a trailer of boiling tar parked behind it. Though it was after hours, the tar was going to be kept hot all night.

Sitting in the Malibu, Rad smelled the boiling tar, mixed with wafts of wood smoke even though it was a June afternoon. A tiny pizza parlor, the only active business on the west side of Main Street, added its greasy smell. Rad wondered where the Chinese Restaurant was going to fit in.

"I wonder if he's dealing drugs or something," she thought. She looked over the town once again, and then glanced down at Joe's paperwork on his seat. The memo from Jackie B. was on top and partially unfolded. She looked at it, looked across the street, looked at the rundown buildings to her right, glanced back down at the memo, and lifted the corner with her unlit cigarette. She glanced back at the

Tattoo Parlor and, seeing no one, opened the memo and read, "The deceased person at the Oil Seep Rez was one of ours, Derek Chang. See what you can find out." It was signed T.dre. So that was where they were headed, to the place where the body had been discovered.

Why the stop at the Tattoo Parlor? What did all this mean? Rad looked at each building in turn as she tried to calm the tension she felt in her neck and behind her eyes. She knew what to do when that build up of tension was coming and took the measures that worked. She unfocused her eyes, relaxed her arms and shoulders, and moved through a progression of self-hypnotic images.

Eventually, Rad got impatient, crossed the highway, wondering to herself why Joe was taking so long. She was annoyed when she entered the vestibule, turned right and was buzzed through the security door, to see Joe, beaming his broad smile. He sent an exaggerated wink her way.

"Radleigh Loonch, these are my friends John and Sue Brown. Folks, this is my new partner in crime. Rad."

The sight before Rad was one from the world of the bizarre. There was Sue standing tall, at six feet, with all of her exposed skin festooned with tattoos of myriad designs in the shades of red, purple, blue, and black. Her hair was magenta; she had a horse face with protruding teeth and jaws, "Prognathism," Rad thought. Oddly, she chose to accentuate the equine theme. Her face was severally pierced with a chain dangling from each ear and a bar with loops at the end protruding three inches on each side of her septum. The ear chains connected to the nose bar to give the impression of the Budweiser Clydesdales. Without the bizarre adornments, Sue would be a plain, extremely slim, but not unattractive woman of thirty-two or three years old.

John Brown was a contrasting case. He was about as broad as he was long and also covered with ink. One got the impression the couple spent their off-work hours decorating each other. He was not a stout mesomorph but a soft and spongy endomorph, with his undraped chest hairless and hanging in folds of flab. To draw attention away from him being an ugly dough ball with no body tone, he had been trying to achieve the arresting look of horns on his head. The ugly lumps were covered by bloody bandages. Rad would later learn from Joe that he was having implants added under his skin a little at a time to give him devil's horns. The scabbing was from the latest incision. The overall impression as they stood side by side, with Sue at six feet and John at five-feet-five inches, was of looking at the number ten on a Satanist calendar.

It occurred to Rad that this whole piercing and tattooing craze represented a drive for individuality in people without the stamina to achieve anything in the way of good or significant works.

Back in the car two towns along the road Radleigh asked, "How can a freak like that help you in the job you're trying to do?"

"Which freak, Sue who has to stand in the same place twice to cast a shadow, or John who would never stop rolling if he tripped walking downhill?" Joe laughed, and then continued, "Ever wonder what people in your profession, archaeology, will think in a few hundred years when they dig up all these people with tatts and piercings and horns—did you see John's working on horns, heh, heh, heh?"

"I studied forensic anthropology and the vicissitudes of the present day are well documented."

"Not after all the books are burned they won't be," Joe knew getting in the last word would aggravate Rad.

"Wha? Anyway, how does a tattooist in a jerk-water rural town give you information to prevent—illegal immigration, drug trafficking, terrorism, whatever?"

Joe Gaspe handed Rad a business card.'

"Tribal Tattoo, Body Art and Piercing with John and Sue," said the darkly somber card. The traffic light changed and Rad accelerated toward the next town. She thought to herself how these towns were so insignificant that many had neither lights nor stop signs. "Just wide spots in the road with slower speed zones."

"What does that card show?" asked Joe.

"Nothing."

Eleven miles down the road they came to a stoplight with a small state route heading off to the left. As they waited for the light to change, Joe pulled a second business card out from under the first. It read, "John Smith, Regional Vice President, Body Art Association of New York State. Tattooists are your friends."

"The Tattoo parlor is like the barbershop of old, a center for news and gossip, perhaps with a rougher crowd, but a link in the chain of information nevertheless."

"So, what did you learn from John Smith?"

"Mel Dumke was through here last week. Other than that, not much."

There weren't many buildings comprising the settlement at the Oil Seep Reservation. Besides the two Smoke Shops, where the Iroquois sold cigarettes and gasoline without the burden of state taxes, there was a community building—hawking bingo and slots—behind the *Empty Blanket Smoke Shop.*" Chief Leonard Brant and an extremely elderly man waited in the Seneca Tribal Police Cruiser.

Joe told Rad to stop and wait in the Malibu. He got out, and walked over to the cruiser. Rad rolled the window down while she smoked. She observed how Joe respectfully stopped and waited to be acknowledged before approaching the cruiser. Joe allowed a short interval of silence. Then Rad heard Joe's familiar laugh, the policeman gave Joe a large manila envelope, then Joe and the old man walked over to Rad's Malibu.

The old man was a very slow walker, not from the obesity and back problems of white Americans, but because he embodied the idea that he was in no hurry to reach the end of his journey. His face was as dark as a black walnut with the uncountable wrinkles of someone who has spent his life either outside in the sun or in a smoky room. Joe opened the front door for him, and he slowly sat down bringing the woodsy smell of a campfire in with him.

"Rad, this is my cousin's Uncle, Joseph Buck Brant, but everybody calls him Uncle Mike."

The sachem turned two luminous eyes on Rad and said, "Your family must be very proud of your great knowledge, women of wisdom will lead us into the future."

Rad mumbled a greeting and looked in the rearview mirror at Joe who was beaming his most disarming smile. Joe said, "Take that road straight ahead and Uncle Mike will help us look over the scene of the crime."

"Crime?" Rad didn't let on that she'd read Joe's note from the FBI agent.

"Yeah, a fellow who was going to be a partner of mine was murdered here ten days ago and the Chief asked me to take Uncle Mike out to look over the spot where the body was found."

"The Real People have always been led by wise women, clan mothers of us all." Uncle Mike's eyes shone brightly as he turned to face Rad.

"How did you know I was…?" She didn't know how to finish the part about forensic anthropology. Somehow she knew that he knew that she was seeing his bones through the emaciated bag of skin that was all there was left of an ancient warrior.

"A man with vision can see things that are there but do not show themselves."

Rad felt tense around this mysterious old man in his green Pendleton shirt, too short khaki trousers, and Bean boots. Her tension was not worry, but a sense of being exposed to something amazing, if unexplainable.

Through a series of turns and switchbacks, their road ascended a small mountain, perhaps two thousand feet in elevation. At one point Uncle Mike asked Rad to stop the car; he rolled down the window and looked toward a roadside ditch. The ditch showed the tracks and drag marks of some vehicle recently pulled out by a tractor. Uncle Mike, who Rad had begun to realize was a Sachem, looked at the ditch, inhaled great wafts of air through his nostrils, closed his eyes, and facing straight at the ditch, hummed quietly and rocked slightly.

Suddenly, he opened his eyes and said. "You can move on."

Rad looked in the rearview mirror before pulling out into the center of the gravel road. She saw Joe Gaspe beaming a grin that seemed to say, " I'm on a great adventure in my life and you should be glad that you're along." Before she turned her eyes back to the road, Joe shot her another exaggerated wink.

Uncle Mike asked that the car be stopped again on a different gravel road, one that was shrouded in a low hanging mist. They were below the dam on a pond called Howard Lake and the mist was rolling off the water down to the roadway. The mist fogged the windshield, and made one have to squint to see things across the road. Joe and the Sachem got out and leaned against the car, looking past a small pond at the wall of the dam. Joe pulled the crime scene eight-by-ten photos out of the envelope. Uncle Mike was staring at a spot, still surrounded by crime scene tape, with his eyes shut.

Uncle Mike spoke, "The poor spirit was killed as a Christian, tortured as a Christian and trussed up and laid out like a Christian, yet he was not one. Nor was he of the people, he was a man from the East. His will to live was great and he still wanders looking for his home place—across the great sea, I believe." The Sachem opened his eyes and accepted Joe's copy of the glossy photo of the body. He nodded, handed the photo back to Joe, and got back in the Malibu. "When you are ready to visit with my friend Father Justin, I am ready."

Joe walked across to the dam accompanied by Rad, who watched closely where she placed her feet in the swampy ground. "He didn't even get close enough to see," she said.

"I guess he saw enough." Joe did not doubt Uncle Mike.

Joe snapped two Polaroid photos of the depression where the body had been removed. It still held the shape of the cross despite some digging by the coroner's people. The beavers had not returned, perhaps because of the amount of man smell or maybe because the dam had not started to leak again.

Joe borrowed Rad's digital camera and took another three shots of the empty depression where the body had been.

The mountaintop where Derek Chang had been found was near the eastern edge of the Oil Seep Reservation. By going down a small saddle and up slightly onto the next mountain, they left the Rez and came upon Mount Isaiah, the retreat of the Franciscan fathers from nearby St. Benedict's College. This mountaintop retreat was a series of scattered cabins and lodges where monks and laypeople could come for contemplation and serenity, away from modern conveniences and distractions. One arrived by car, but there was no electricity, no phone, simple meals were cooked with wood or propane and offered to penitents and visitors alike.

When Rad's Malibu pulled up, the dinner bell was sounding, drawing in the people from the outlying cabins. Rad, Joe, and Uncle Mike entered the dining room and Father Justin greeted them effusively. He obviously knew Joe and the Sachem well and turned his twinkling Irish eyes on Rad and sparkled at her throughout the introduction—Joe was a very polite person and never failed to introduce Rad to the members of his network.

They were seated and before they ate their plain fare, fish and soup and bread, Father Justin took his place at the head of the table and led a short prayer. He ate quietly with the Franciscans.

"An Irish charmer, that," Rad said between bites of bread.

"He's Polish, the brogue is a put up job." Joe had a way of gently deflating Rad, who had been feeling good about the sincere attention of both Uncle Mike and Father Justin.

Uncle Mike slurped a spoonful of soup and said. "All of you are Irish, and Polish, and English, and French, you People of the Sunrise."

After the meal, when the other diners had returned to their meditations or labors, the Father brought a tray with a teapot to the table and poured tea for Rad, Joe, and himself. He gave a different beverage to Uncle Mike, strong black coffee. Rad watched the Sachem ladle spoonful after spoonful of sugar into his coffee. He saw her watching and gave her a wide smile, opening a mouth that contained only one tooth—the left front—ironically the front tooth that Joe Gaspe was missing.

"You whites ruined us with your Bible and your guns and your firewater and your smallpox but you did the most damage with sugar—can't resist my sweets." He laughed out loud at that, tasted his coffee, and ladled in another spoonful of sugar.

"Ms. Loonch, I have known Uncle Mike for many years and he consults here at Mount Isaiah during our multi-cultural retreat weekends, as well as at other times. Joe Gaspe has asked both of us to be part of his network of people who try to prevent attacks on our civilization. You and he are here for the advice and expertise of both Uncle Mike and me in our areas of specialization."

"Thank you Father, Joe doesn't tell me much," replied Rad.

"Forgive him, young lady, but he is in a position of great danger to himself and to all his interlocutors. The fewer details he shares, the less danger he puts us in and the more freedom he has to prevent crimes."

"If you tell the boss too much stuff—supply too many details—he gets confused and can't do anything to help." Joe said this as he spread the Polaroids, and crime scene glossies before Father Justin on the table. He held out his hand and Rad turned on her digital camera and placed it in his hand. The four were silent while the good Father put on his half glasses and examined the items. Uncle Mike, done with his sugar solution, closed his eyes and hummed slightly.

Father Justin went through all the items twice and held the Polaroids up to the evening light coming through the stained glass window around the mosaic image of Christ. Rad tried to see this from his perspective; being of a Protestant faith she was both repelled and fascinated by the Catholic's reliance on bloody images of their savior. She assumed that the suffering of Christ was more graphic for them than it was for Lutherans.

"Joe, there is evil in the world. This is the work of the devil himself." Father Justin was emphatic.

Nodding his head, Joe said, "Go on."

"Satan does his work through men, but he is behind a crime like this."

"What makes you say that, the layout of the body?"

"There are auras in these pictures, the fires of Hell have burned this shape into the beaver dam, and those who did this do not even have free will. They are controlled by the beast."

"These were not Iroquois. There are young radicals around here," he gestured to the western mountain at the edge of the Rez, "but they did not do this."

"I agree, our people did not participate," said Uncle Mike.

Joe looked at Uncle Mike, then at Father Justin, and raised one eyebrow in a gesture of inquiry.

"Uncle Mike and I do not disagree on many things, Cuban cigars perhaps. We do not discuss theology to avoid argument. How do I know it was not a member of the tribe? One, why would people of the longhouse leave the body on their home ground? Two, they would suspect that an Asian person may not be a Christian? Three, what good is a symbol in an out of the way place—the body would have made the newspapers in almost any other location. Fourth, this was a warning meant for whites and Iroquois and Asians and everyone else."

"You believe it was the rag heads who did this?"

"Islamists, Joe, or Islamofascists if you prefer—not all Arabs are terrorists, far from it," Father Justin continued. "I believe that there is a powerful and truly evil force behind the terror network and that the Chinese Communist People's Liberation Army through Islamic Terror Groups are the agents of this evil. My deduction is that the young Chinese American was killed, or at least brought here, by other ethnic Chinese."

"A Chinese gang war?"

"No, their enemy is the US and its commitment to individual freedom. It just happened that the US agent was of Chinese ethnicity. Not by coincidence, I might add."

"How did you know he was a government asset?"

Uncle Mike spoke during a pause, too polite to interrupt and too calm to hurry into the breach, he nevertheless took the opening offered by the Father. "The idea of using a Chinese to spy on the

Chinese was too obvious. I worry that now they know that there is a member of the Real People looking at them," his eyes were boring into Joe with a piercing quality that Rad concluded was different from the luminous energy she had noticed before. "Their need to kill may sweep over our tribal home and harm our people, Joe."

Joe knew that Uncle Mike had no fear for himself but was protective of younger members of the tribe.

"Somebody knew the Rez and a little woodcraft here, though they did not know that the beavers would bury their symbol." Joe was getting an image of what had happened.

"Are you thinking that this was Mel Dumke?" Rad asked Joe.

"If the authorities know the name of an agent of the evil lord why do they not arrest him?" Father Justin asked. Uncle Mike nodded; confirming that he also thought that evil was afoot.

"They hope that I can use Dumke to find the person in power behind the terror, at least locally." Joe gathered up his photos.

Father Justin gently grasped his wrist. "Joe, you must be careful. Before you go I want you to meet someone."

Father Justin led the other three down across a field, over a rill brimming with watercress, and up a small rise to where a man was standing beside a tractor and harrow at the edge of a freshly turned five acre field.

"Joe Smokes, meet Joe Gaspe and Radleigh Loonch. This is Joseph Smokes—he pulled that landscape truck and trailer out of the ditch with his tractor," Father Justin said.

The man was a Native American; dressed as a cowboy on top he had on a western style shirt—well worn—and dressed as a military veteran on the bottom. He wore a pair of fatigue pants bloused at the cuff and tucked into scuffed combat boots. He had short legs, a flat butt, and a long torso topped by a big head. Rad noticed this because her anthropology studies had made her see a person's bone structure when she met him. His crew cut, of coarse black hair, was cut in the Marine style. An angry white scar line ran from front to back along the left side of his head; the scar was vivid against his sun-browned skin. He nodded to Joe and Rad and spoke briefly to Uncle Mike in his native language.

Father Justin explained, "Joseph works for us on the farming and food production here at the Mount; he rides his tractor back and forth to the Rez, as he is not in possession of a state driver's license. Joe is a former Marine who was wounded in the first Gulf War. He was shot with a glancing blow in the head and has lost some of his cognitive ability. He can no longer read—but is a master with vegetables and grains. Right Joseph?"

Rad noticed how Joe Smokes twitched. He moved his head and left shoulder like a man looking back for a pursuer, but turned back quickly as if he'd seen nothing.

"Effin' slopes, in effin' suits, eff me, eff them too!"

"Tourrette's syndrome is one effect of his wound," explained Father Justin.

"So these were Asians in the landscape truck?' asked Gaspe.

"Effin gooks, slopes. Slant-eyes!" He held his index fingers besides his eyes and stretched them quickly before he twitched again. "One white devil—two slopes. Not a Marine – too soft. Effin slopes! Eff me, eff them."

"Were these the guys that left the body up at Howard Lake?"

"Eff yes, muddy shoes. It was them! He was Navy. Effin swabby."

"Joseph did not lose the colorful language of the Marine Corps with his injury." Turning to the man, Father Justin said, "Thank you Joseph, you've been a big help."

Joseph turned away with several twitches and continued to mutter "eff them, eff me" to himself.

"Excuse me, Joseph, was there anything on the truck, any writing or pictures? What color was it?" Joe Gaspe asked.

"Effin' truck was red. Effin' hop toads on it. Effin' stupid lookin' hop toads."

"Serving in the white man's military is bad for Real People. His wound has made him forget how to read the English taught in Government Schools. But his brush with death has allowed his ancestors to teach him an old version of our language. His mind has fallen but he has picked up his aksotha's, or grandmother's, mind." Uncle Mike explained how the pathos of Joseph Smokes' condition was not total.

"It could be that the logo of the landscaping company had a stylized frog drawn in it." Rad was trying to help.

"I wonder if he's right?" Gaspe said this aloud as they walked back toward the Malibu.

"He knows." Uncle Mike said this with such conviction that Joe and Rad both knew he was right.

"Those with Moneto in their head know much. We must heed them."

"I suppose." Joe thought for a minute, then said, "There is no way he could know that Mel Dumke was ex-Navy."

"He saw it in him."

"Nine pieces won't scare anybody, let's get fifteen." Joe Gaspe was hungry.

"I'll only need two or three, so get what you want." Rad wanted to get back to Pantherville, though she was hungry, too. They'd stopped at the fried chicken takeout restaurant in Dover Corners— the central commercial district for several of the nearby small towns.

Walking back to the Malibu, they had to cross Route 16. Rad was thinking about Joe and his appetites and how unlike a stereotype of a Native American he was. The opposite of a stoic, he was an enthusiast. He liked everything and plenty of it.

After checking for traffic, he double-timed it across the highway.

"Hey, watch out!" someone yelled from Joe's right. Rad looked to see a man shaking his fist at a blue short bus that came squealing out of the driveway of Pearl's restaurant. It took the corner so fast that it was briefly on two wheels. The bus came back to vertical with a rocking motion and the driver poured the gas to her. There was Joe, ahead of Rad, contentedly munching a chicken leg with the same hand he was carrying his take out order. Because of the chicken bucket, he couldn't see the blue bus, picking up speed, hurtling straight at him.

Rad, having stopped to light a cigarette, and was well behind Joe.

She saw the driver hunch his shoulders forward as he barreled down the lane next to the parked Malibu. Thoughts sped through her mind. "Couldn't Joe hear the roar as the diesel engine wound up toward top speed? Was he smacking and chewing and gulping and mmm-mming too loud to hear?"

"Hey Joe! Look out!" Rad yelled as loud as she could. Joe turned back, with that chicken leg in his mouth endways. He started to wave when the skrreeekk, skreeekk of a red tail hawk caused Joe to look up. The shadow of the hawk's wingspan, huge over his gaze, the waving and pointing from Rad, and the shouts of other spectators caught his attention. He turned left and saw the vehicle bearing down on him. Now that he'd turned halfway around, his take-out bucket no longer blocked his view. Joe saw his impending doom. He bent his knees while throwing his arms up and back. He did a backwards-leaping Fosbury flop onto the hood of Rad's car. The bucket of chicken flew into the air and bounced off the blue bus's grill and rolled up the windshield, as the vehicle whooshed past within an inch of the Malibu, spewing chicken along the road for twenty feet.

"Mister, mister, are you all right?" the man, who had been nearly hit in the driveway of Pearl's, came running up.

"I'm OK." Joe was looking at the receding blue back of the short bus.

"Did anybody see the license plate on that bus?"

"It was smeared with mud—not visible," said another concerned citizen.

"Joe, Joe are you ok?" Rad ran up to him.

"I'm all right but I'm going to remain hungry," Joe said looking at his fourteen chicken pieces beginning to form grease spots along the pavement.

It took another hour to reach the Park & Ride where Rad would drop Joe off, near his home. Rad and Joe were each wrapped in their own thoughts.

✸ ✱ ✸

"That was an attempt on Joe's life I just witnessed. I wonder if he knows what danger he is in. I wonder if I'm in equal danger. He seems to be reveling in this. Look at him.

"What is it about men? If he was twenty years younger I might be interested. He's not hot or anything but he has that element of danger. For thousands of years, no, make that millions of years, women have depended on men for protection from other men. A man who is physical, powerful, and brave represents the safety that only a dangerous man can provide. It would be better if it were not so. I would have made the world different if it were up to me, but drawing cards against a hand that is a sure winner won't change the outcome. I try to use my emotions as information but not let them control my life. My instinct for survival is most effective when matched with a man's instincts." Rad was used to analyzing herself and her mental processes as she was doing now, from an anthropological perspective.

"But his habits! He eats so much and most of it is fat or meat. He's like a machine. Men are so hairy and stinky, what is it that attracts us? Still, if he weren't so old and so married.

"I wonder what his wife is like. I hope she doesn't think I'm after him. I don't want any married man or one with kids. Still, if he was younger and single." Rad had grown to understand about men and their challenges; the natural world of fishing and hunting, danger, difficult puzzles. They loved this stuff. If it put demands on their strength, resourcefulness, or ingenuity then they wanted to do it. The feeling of accomplishment provided by challenges, like this job for Agent Andre, and the difficulties of musky fishing, was what men lived for. Sure, a home and a hearth, wife and kids, was a good place to rest, but put them on the trail with a problem and they were really happy.

❄ ✳ ❄

Joe was aware that his life had been threatened but he put it out of his mind. "I sure wanted to take the wrinkles out of my stomach," he said.

The thought that he'd just been nearly killed got in line behind the thought that he was hungry. Joe's mind worked that way. He put an idea in the back and let it roll around for a while, sometimes for a long while. He thought of himself as neither wise nor shrewd but he could use what he had, doggedness, stamina, and an unwillingness to let ideas fade away. An idea may lie dormant but it would not go away.

He was a curious man and by knowing what he did not know—having no illusions—he was blessed, or cursed, with a mind that wanted to learn what he needed to know.

He thought about this new and dangerous job, of which he had told his wife, Kate, nothing. In many ways he took his children for granted. Each new girl was just another plate at the table. He had all the stuff, the clothes, the strollers, and the changing table. But then there was Amelia, a girl who had grown up on him. She had her own independent mind and it was very independent. Now was payback time for Joe who'd given his parents multiple migraines.

Kids eventually became people in their own right. They had dreams and ambitions. As people, they were affected by numerous factors that Joe could not control. He wanted to impress his eldest daughter that he wasn't a total screw-up. But was that a good reason to put his life on the line and risk the well-being of the little ones?

Then there was his responsibility to Kate. She had kept him through all his irresponsible behavior. She was a terrific mother to the girls. She knew how to keep him on a long leash if not under the porch.

In the end, Joe knew he was going to stay with the job for Agent Andre. He was a man who kept driving and kept trying to improve his own estimate of himself. Good sense suggested he give up this dangerous business he was not trained for. He was not young enough for it, he was too obvious, too much of a bull. Yet he knew he would drive ahead. It was what he did.

Agent Andre

Chapter 5

June 20

M arv was impressed with the new boat that Joe Gaspe said was a loaner. It was a twenty-one-foot Boston Whaler, with twin 185 Mercury four stroke outboards.

"Marvelous," he shouted as they flew up the river toward the opening day fishing tournament in Pantherville Harbor. Dawn was just breaking in the east and the water was turning from black iron to gray steel, pewter, copper, and brass where the slight chop bent the light.

Joe had had the boat for two weeks, since being turned back at the bridge while trying to fish Ontario's musky season opener. He'd been busy with other things and hadn't had a chance to show it to his fishing partner. They'd discussed it over a few beers, but this was Marv's maiden voyage.

The boat was up on plane creating minimum friction and leaving a perfect symmetrical wake as it cruised at forty mph on the way to the Upper Lake. The seven-mile trip takes ten minutes at that speed. Wind washing his face, Marv was beaming, looking around, and laughing out loud.

"Aren't you afraid to take your boat into Canada anymore?" Marv shouted, louder than he had to. The four stroke motors made much less noise than the usual two-stroke outboards.

"Reluctant, not afraid." Joe spoke loudly but did not need to shout. "We've come to an understanding, Ontario and me." Joe had that familiar twinkle in his eye that telegraphed, to those who knew him, that whatever he said was slathered with irony.

It was not Joe's habit to keep things from Marv. To his wife, he could only reveal selected snatches of his agenda. He flattered himself to think that was for her safety—true now, but Joe had always had a life apart from his wife and daughters. He had become adept at compartmentalizing information. He was practiced at telling only what needed to be told and causing little uproar with the omissions. But, Marv, never the moralist, usually knew whatever Joe was doing.

Marv did not yet know about the network Joe was establishing, nor his secret mission—though he would need to know eventually— nor that Joe was not really working on a big project for a homebuilder in Pantherville. Marv had steady work with a roofing company in Muskedaigua. Since construction workers work at least a half-day on Saturdays, they only got together on Sundays to fish and on an occasional evening for beers. When they both had worked in construction in the same housing development, Marv had been driving Joe to work— Joe's license was suspended for driving under the influence. Now, with Joe working in Pantherville, Marv dropped him at a Park & Ride where he got picked up every morning to go work at his supposed big housing project.

Marv wondered how Joe could have this nifty boat and not have even a rudimentary automobile, but it was opening day for musky fishing, he was out with his best friend, and they were skimming along toward the fish grounds, what could be better? A man likes anticipation in his hobby, a sense of more to come, even if the more is never as much as he hopes. What was it Melvin Loonch said? "Hope is just postponed disappointment." If the catching of fish were needed to enjoy the sport—if it were required to feed the family or fulfill the goal—then fishing would be a great source of frustration. But, fishing, musky fishing anyway, does not require the catching of fish. It requires time on the water pursuing the quarry—sometimes not even pursuing very hard. The effort is the reward.

Marv was shaken from his reverie when the Border Patrol pulled alongside and paralleled the Whaler with their patrol boat. Joe slowed down to about five miles per hour when given a hand signal. The patrol boat was running twin Honda four stroke outboards and with Joe's two cruising at five miles per hour, the noise was low enough that they were able to hold a shouted conversation.

"Anyone below?" The officer indicated the cuddy cabin of Joe's boat with a nod of his head.

"Just us two this morning!"

"Where you going?"

"Pantherville Harbor. Musky fishing. Opening day."

"Have a nice day!" With that shout, the patrol boat peeled off and headed back downriver.

Marv shook his head. United States Customs and Border Patrol Agents had just interviewed them, while in Canadian waters. There were a lot of questions today for Marv. Gaspe turned the Whaler east and headed for his favorite trolling run.

When they had started musky fishing, Joe and Marv had chartered trips with captains, Magnus Markson and Slim Tomkins, to learn their runs. Without a GPS system Joe used landmarks and a compass to memorize his patterns for trolling the north end of Pantherville Harbor. They headed towards Chinaman's light. Obsolete now, it was a sight to see, a decorative lighthouse from two centuries back that had been used when the breakwalls were being constructed by the Chinese laborers. Those coolies had suffered great hardship and loss of life to build the longest breakwall in the world at that time.

By pointing the bow at this landmark Joe was able to scrape (troll closely beside) the backside of two breakwalls that were known to hold bait pods and therefore predators.

The harbor breakwalls were situated perpendicular to the track of the prevailing wind. This meant they broke the waves effectively when the wind was out of the west or off that prevailing direction by up to a quarter of the compass. With wind from the southwest, west, or northwest there was a dead spot at the north end of the walls. Bait held there, just off the rock piles. This bait, circling in a revolving pod shaped like an amoeba, could conserve energy while feeding on the plankton suspended there. Similarly the predator species could feast, with reduced energy expenditure, on the bait. There was a slight oscillating movement east and west of this slack water section. The famous Captain Slim Tomkins had developed a trolling pass that would sweep through all possible locations of bait off these walls. Joe followed Slim's run as it dovetailed into the well-known big fish area at the end of Dennehey's wall. Here again, the prevailing wind stacked the bait and the predators.

From Dennehey's, Tomkin's run took a dog bone course down into the Red Rock Canal, one hundred seventy degrees back to the main harbor, skirted a huge weed bed, and ran one hundred seventy degrees back down the adjacent Pantherville River. Then a loop was made to turn back out toward the harbor and cross the shadow of Chinaman's light, which Marv called the Taliban Temple for some unknown reason—perhaps because he had usually been hung over in social studies class—and the run ended up scraping the breakwall at the Coast Guard slip.

A musky trolling run requires both precision and creativity. There is a need to scrape the drop-offs closely, but also several options where side trips can be taken to explore for the existence of bait pods. or tickle the edges of weedbeds in various locations. Muskies set up on prime fishing spots and don't move often. Twice a day some of the muskies get up and cruise, hunting for additional food. These roaming, searching, feeding fish are the likeliest to be caught. Most of the time, muskies camp out on a spot and only eat what is delivered to their doorstep. These fish can be aggravated into biting by precision trolling or accurate casting or jigging.

Joe and Marv were creatures of ceremony and liked to start off their trolling with two complete, forward and back circuits of the Tomkins run before they branched off to other trolls. One of the advantages the musky gains by its behavior is that fishermen, being grown-up little boys, can't stay still long enough to be precise or thorough on these trolls and their impatience mitigates against success.

The mid-June start of musky season meant that the weather was amenable to all kinds of boaters. After Joe and Marv had made two turns at the entrance to the Pantherville River, sailboats began to parade out from their moorings, like lambs following a lead goat. Once the sailors started, there were always a few coming or going. Joe was only able to ply a north-south troll of lesser promise.

"Give them a wide berth," Marv said, because the sailboat under canvas has the right of way over powerboats using motor power.

"When they use their engine they are motorboats and are no better than us." Joe was cranky because he wanted to hit Tomkin's run once more.

"The less maneuverable boat has the right of way. You know that. When they are running their motor and raising their sails they have priority over us in two ways, size and type of locomotion." Marv stated the rule just to aggravate Joe.

" Let's take a couple of outer loops and see what happens." Joe resigned himself to the loss of the Tomkins run for today.

Cutting across from the front, south side of the short wall toward the back of the lighthouse wall, they were surprised by the Coast Guard Patrol Boat that roared up beside them and slowed to trolling speed.

"Remove the fishing rods from your port side and heave to." An officer spoke through a bullhorn.

"This must be our day for cops. Bastards," said Marv. Joe throttled back into neutral and the four rods were reeled in and stowed as the patrol boat sidled up to Joe's Whaler and bumped its pontoon into the gunwale.

"Do we have your permission to come aboard and conduct a courtesy inspection?" The officer in charge had perfected the bureaucratic government speak that combined politeness and threat to make an offer that couldn't be refused. Permission denied to the Coasties meant a daylong nitpicking hassle that would spoil any fishing. The courtesy thing was also a misnomer since they would fine a boat or send it to port for any violation.

Four guardsmen were on the patrol boat. A pilot was at the wheel idling the twin Honda four stroke outboard motors, that were so quiet that they didn't even interfere with conversation. The captain had the bullhorn, unneeded with the boats tied together, and instructed Joe in what was to happen. A mate had attached a line to one of the Whaler's cleats and was standing at the ready, hand poised over his sidearm. Another mate, the inspector, was waiting for Marv to hook up the lure on the last rod and move it to the starboard side before he boarded. All carried side arms, wore life jackets, and kept their expressions bland.

"Please produce your flares and fire extinguisher." Joe reached into a compartment and showed both items. The guardsman on board inspected the dates of expiration.

"Operate your blower for us." Joe complied.

"I see you have two people on board. Show us two appropriate personal flotation devices, if you will." All conversation came from the captain, not a word came from the man poking around on board. Joe was in compliance with the jackets.

"Please operate your horn." Joe gave it a toot. "Now, if you would show us your cuddy cabin." Joe opened the hatch and the man on board stuck his head down the companionway and looked for what was not there. Joe lit a cigarette trying not to shake or show any nervousness.

"We need to see a copy of your registration, please." Joe produced his papers.

"If you have a paddle we will be finished with this inspection." Joe held up his pathetic three-foot long paddle that conformed to regulations but would be absolutely useless in moving the boat.

"Everything is in order. While this certificate," The guardsman on board had filled out a form in triplicate and he handed the yellow copy to Joe, " will not exempt you from future inspections, if you show it to the officer of another Coast Guard boat doing an inspection, they may be able to save time."

"Thanks, officer." Marv was playing up to power.

"Have a nice day." The patrol boat moved ahead to inspect another fishing boat that was coming along off Joe's starboard bow.

Joe advanced his throttles and said, "Whew, let's troll. It's a good thing we offloaded all those illegal aliens earlier, eh?" Marv didn't think this was funny.

They had gone out into the lake and looped around back toward the harbor when they were approached by another boat. This one was festooned with a banner saying "Mayor's Harbor Team" and had a news cameraperson on the bow. The Mayor's Boat lined up to intercept the Whaler. As they approached, a permed and primped young woman with a microphone hailed the boat.

"May we speak with you, please? Mayor Anthony would like to ask you a few questions." The local reporter, a telegenic beauty named Lisa Liska, was looking beachy in a contrived way and gave Joe and Marv the Queen wave as the two boats neared each other.

"Aw, crap. We're gonna have to pull the rods in again." Marv was frustrated. It was eleven thirty now and the waterways were crowded. The temperature had risen to the point where cold-blooded people would be out, and Mayor Tony Anthony came around to smile and wave to Joe and Marv as they hove-to and re-stowed their musky rods.

The reporter greeted the boys effusively and introduced the Mayor. He was a former basketball player, too tall and landlubberly to be comfortable in a boat. He'd been Mayor for four terms but was most famous for scoring 34 points against Duke in a losing game twenty-four years before. The operator of the Mayor's boat was not as skilled as the Coast Guardsman and the boats bumped hard as they came alongside. This caused the Mayor to fall half into the Whaler and the reporter keeled over with a little scream. Marv helped Mayor Anthony right himself while Joe gently caught Lisa Liska. He took the opportunity to admire her modest but well-tanned topside.

Lisa stood straight with a big stage smile and said into the camera, "We're here with Mayor Anthony as he greets some of the people using what is known locally as Pantherville's number one asset, the waterfront. Mr. Mayor."

"Thank you Lisa, I'd just like to say what a marvelous day it is and how great it is to see people from all over the western tier using the fabulous waters of our lake and river. Where are you boys from?"

"Muskedaigua."

"All the way from Muskedaigua, isn't that nice. And what are you doing to enjoy the harbor on this fine Saturday morning?"

"We were fishing." This came from Marv. He was the one Lisa was pointing the microphone towards. Her eyes, however, were on Joe, who was beaming his best smile and had a business card for his rod building business held out to her. She glanced around and furtively pocketed the card.

"Ah, fishing, one of my favorite pastimes," the Mayor lied. "What kind of fishing are you doing?"

"We were musky fishing, a little bit." Marv wasn't disguising his lack of enthusiasm for this. Meanwhile Joe had let his hand caress Lisa Liska's slender upper arm as the boats gently rocked beside each other. She didn't move away.

"Oh, I love musky for my Friday night fish fry," said the Mayor.

"We don't eat muskies and our club discourages the killing of any."

The producer of the news team interrupted. He waved at Lisa and the Mayor saying, "Cut, cut, that's enough of that."

Joe gave Lisa one of his exaggerated winks and chuckled as the boats floated apart. Lisa tapped her pants pocket that held the business card.

"Let's talk to a jet ski operator, next." The Mayor's mind was already on other things.

"Phony bastard never fished in his life, I'll bet." Marv was ticked off.

"What did you expect?" Joe lifted his fingers to his nose and inhaled the scent of Lisa Liska.

The trolling on opening day gets difficult when the weather is nice. Too many sailors, jet skiers, power boaters, and others are thrashing about to make precise or even presentable runs. Marv and Joe went the rest of the day without catching any fish.

They slept in Marv's truck camper bed that night and Joe had one of his power dreams. This was a dream where he met his cousin Mo Snow in the ether and they dreamed together, though they were miles apart. Mo was not at the reservation in Kahnawake but just across the Straits in Ontario. He was also fishing for muskies on opening weekend. He was also sleeping that night in a friend's camper.

Since their days on the warrior's barricade at Oka in 1990, Mo and Joe had learned how to meet in their dreams and travel together via their dream bodies in the spirit world. They did not need to be nearby to travel through sky, sea, or land while dreaming together.

Joe lay down his head in the bed of Marv's pickup truck with the smell of sweaty feet flowering the space. He concentrated on his vision of Lisa Liska while sliding into a reverie. Joe's preference for women who were round here and there over the boyish bony ideal of the early twenty-first century did not stop him from considering all women likely. But the dream world has images of its own to share and follows its own agenda.

Joe is of the Wolf clan but his totem animal is the red-tailed hawk. It was on the wings of a hawk that he now rose into the air and saw a raven leading the way south. Soon, they were high enough to cover many miles on the wing. The hawk and raven were joined in flight by a heron, slowly flapping its long wings. Mo Snow was of the Wolf clan as well, but his totem was the heron, a bird that could keep pace with a speeding boat using lazy strokes of its wings.

Mo and Joe looked at each other as the earth disappeared beneath their southward progress. It was mere moments later that the raven urged the heron to glide down to earth. After several more minutes the raven nodded and the hawk went into a perpendicular-cliff steep-accelerating-ninety mile per hour-dive into a clearing in a tropical forest. There in a nearby pool stood the heron that was Mo Snow. Joe, the hawk, was perched on a snaggy dead tree just above the wading pool. The heron and hawk eyed each other. At the same time Joe told Mo without words, "Mind the frogs, they are poison," and Mo returned with, "The red newt is a deadly eft."

Joe saw that the heron had scared the frogs from the pond and they hopped, colorful and shimmering red yellow blue, in all directions. The heron's instinct to spear a frog for a meal was checked only by Mo using all his willpower.

The hawk sat on the tree, his sharp eye on the leaf litter below, where an eft, as big as a hellbender, slithered over and under the damp leaves, alternately showing itself and hiding. The hawk's instinct to pounce and rip and tear was held in check by the might of Joe's willpower.

Joe looked at Mo when the raven croaked three times. They knew it was this trickster who had brought them to the brink of poison food and held them back as well. When Joe looked at the frogs lined up on the bank and crawling up the trees, he saw Mel Dumke's face and, for the first time, he was sure that it had been Dumke that had attempted to run him over with the blue bus. Mo looked at the red newt now fully exposed beneath Joe and saw an Asian face with black eyes, stony and cold, in the hot tropical forest.

The raven croaked three more times, calling the heron and hawk to join it circling higher and higher, heading north away from poison meals and certain death in a strange land.

Joe didn't only dream at night while sleeping. He often grasped an image from those night dreams and worked it over in daylight. Through relaxation techniques learned in one of the many times that he quit smoking, he could re-enter a dream to carry the image or action to another plateau.

Joe would sit or lie quietly in a dark place and, beginning with his toes and moving up, he relaxed each successive part of his body until he entered a dream state. The last image before relaxation would be the starting place for further dreaming. He often started with the well-turned nymphomaniacs of his imagination, but usually his most pressing dream image would take over.

He'd had a recurring image in the real (dream) world of leaving his house to fish for muskies. On his way out of his house he would pass two Franklin silver half dollars, stacked on top of each other, about to fall off the edge of a chair. In passing, Joe would straighten the stack and move on. He was puzzled as to the meaning of this in his dreams and tried several times to work it out in day-dreaming. Always the two large coins, bigger than halves, even bigger then silver dollars, were slipping; always Joe restacked, always he moved on to go fishing; sometimes he saw another figure watching him from the shadows.

The repeated image of such a short sequence in a dream left Joe knowing that there was more.

Chapter 6

June 23rd

The Tuesday night sailboat race was in full swing when Joe Gaspe and Marv Ankara turned into Pantherville Harbor. They were going to cast for muskies and pike behind Dennehey's wall. Marv had Wednesday off and the plan was to fish until late, sleep on the boat, and fish most of the day Wednesday. The pike that could be caught were small compared to their regular quarry, muskies, but they could be had in numbers and fishing was more fun when you caught something. Marv didn't know it, but Joe had another thing on his mind because of a phone call he'd received earlier in the day.

The predominant white sails were mingled with multi-colored ones, some with logos and some with advertising, at the start of the sailboat race. The boats raced according to class. This meant that there were multiple races going on at any one time. To the untrained eye of a power boater, it looked like chaos. Some boats had turned by a nearer destination buoy and started back for the harbor on the first of two laps while other, larger, boats legged it out for the farther marker on their only lap. The wind was light and puffy, and several boats, piloted by inexperienced sailors, were losing way and having boom shifts as they struggled. A boom shift occurs when the pilot steers too close to the wind and gets it on the wrong side of his bow. The sail, no longer full of wind, luffs and flutters until the boom —the horizontal spar—swings from one side of the boat to the other. This maneuver can be dangerous to those in the boat since the boom can smack a crewmember or knock one overboard.

The leaders in the race were always bunched together as they competed week-to-week to be the best in their class. There was also a large group of sailors who wanted to do well—have a good sail—but were competing only against themselves. While competent, they were not particularly competitive. There was another group of the less skilled, still learning, crews who completed the course with some degree of difficulty but generally knew what they were doing. There was also a group of wannabes who couldn't sail well at all and added a level of confusion to the scene that seemed to Joe to be an aggravation to the real racers.

To the casual observer the sight was one of great beauty as the boats, many of them stunning, with their colorful taut sails, sliced this way and that across the horizon. Joe and Marv had seen it before and Marv paid no attention. Joe was being observant this evening. They snuck around the eastern edge of the racing boats and tucked into the Red Rock Canal to start their casting.

The canal is dredged for the commercial traffic of days past and has shallow weed beds at its edges that are loaded with small fish. The small fish attract pike and muskies in the early season when the water is still cool. A slight breeze from the west-southwest moved their boat along as Joe and Marv threw lures up onto the weedy flats and brought them back over the edge to the deeper channel. Many small fish, pike and bass, would slap the lures on the flats, some missing and some being caught. The bigger fish were on the break line where the depth dropped abruptly to twenty-four feet. Joe hoped that the little fish on the flats would miss his offering so that he had a chance at the bigger fish on the break line.

Evenings were long at this time of year and it never really got fully dark. Marv and Joe were chucking lures at a leisurely pace, saving their strength for the long haul that would be their all-nighter. The breeze pushed them north up the canal. They used their electric motor to assist the drift and move along the canal, casting lures. They neared the yacht club and then passed it. Their boat had drifted near the canal wall and the boats moored at the CPO's Club.

"Let's troll towards the gap. Maybe we can get a pass in before the sailor girls come back."

They stowed the casting rods. Marv set out trolling rods with crank baits while Joe started one of the outboards and headed slowly up the west side of the Red Rock Canal. They were slightly more than one mile from the start of their drift so it took them twenty-five minutes to get to the north end of the Pantherville Harbor. They passed one boat limping back toward the Yacht Club, its sail limp and flapping like a shirttail.

This was the night of the women's race so Marv and Joe closely checked out any crew that they passed in the boat. Everyone on the crews didn't have to be a woman for the boat to participate, but the captain and pilot had to be female. It was a cool evening with a modest breeze so there was no exposed flesh to yield to the boys' prying eyes, yet they looked. Some men try to deny their visual nature, but Marv and Joe gloried in indulging their appreciation of the female form.

Joe began a trolling circuit of the Tomkin's run when his boat reached the gap. There was only one sailboat inside the walls and it was headed down the Pantherville River toward the moorings at the sailboat basin. Instead of running down the river on its engine power, the boat was tacking against the wind. The river at that point is only one hundred yards wide, so tacking back and forth uses the whole width and then some, making for a probable and unnecessary traffic jam. Joe approached the river entrance from the north. The sailboat was trying to go east by tacking northeast and southeast alternately.

"There's a woman that doesn't know what she's doing, doesn't understand the rules of the road on the water and doesn't care about anyone else." Joe was talking to Marv who was in the back corner cleaning weeds off a lure and setting it back out.

"What did you say, partner?"

"I said, this babe doesn't know how to sail."

"Since when do babes have beards and wear turbans? Look at the crew." Marv waved at the cockpit. The pilot at the wheel was beardless but appeared to be a boy in his early teens. Meanwhile the "crew" sat huddled close together in the back. Each of them wore a white robe, a full beard, and a turban. No one in this crew was doing anything to help with sailing the boat. There were too many people for the space and those not staring straight ahead were glancing side to side as if pursued. One gray beard jabbered rapidly at the poor young pilot, berating him. Joe didn't get the impression that this was an English speaker.

"Marv, gimme your cell!" Marv handed the phone to Joe. He dialed and steered at the same time. The Whaler was gaining on the floundering sailboat and Joe needed to swing away to avoid a collision. He got a good look at the crew—no women involved. He was able to hear the old man hectoring louder and louder at the pilot—definitely not English.

Joe's first attempted call, to the operator who was supposed to be on duty 24/7, failed to connect. Marv's phone needed a charge. He grabbed his ship-to-shore radio.

Tuned to channel 16, he said, "Coast Guard Pantherville, this is Dr. Dento, do you copy?"

The Guard operator came back, "This is Coast Guard Station Pantherville, please identify yourself."

"This is Dr. Dento, a private vessel, can you switch to channel twenty?"

"Coast Guard Station Pantherville, switching to twenty."

Joe dialed up and heard, "Go ahead Dr. Demo."

" That's Dr. Dento! Coast Guard, there's a boat out here in the Pantherville River that you need to check out. It's all wrong. Looks like illegal immigration to me."

"Dr Demo, we will investigate. Be advised, do not approach the vessel."

"Dento out." Joe looked up to see the Coast Guard patrol boat motoring out of their slip just ahead. Marv pointed down the river as the patrol boat roared past toward the now badly floundering sailboat. The Guard made no acknowledgement of the Whaler.

"Stupid Pakis, don't know how to sail their boat, don't know when to pass the Coasties, and don't know that American women don't have beards. Sheesh!" Marv said. Joe and Marv lost concentration on their fishing as they watched the Guard stop the boat.

The sailboat didn't heave-to until the patrol's sidearms and several rifles were trained on them.

"If they don't get these people before they land, they can get lawyers and tie us up in court for years. Before they land, the Coast Guard can just send them back to their country of origin. Of course, they'll try again next week." Joe was showing off his knowledge of the Homeland Security bureaucracy.

"What happens to the boat?" Marv asked.

"If they can find the owner, he'll probably have some explaining to do. Otherwise it will get auctioned off in a few years."

The health teacher, an earnest young woman with a blank smiling face, was droning on about self-esteem as if she were a guard lecturing the prisoners. She taught the subject, and why it was especially important for girls, as if self-esteem was something you could put on, like a light jacket on a chilly evening. Amelia Gaspe had briefly considered asking her a question, but had demurred because she had no confidence that this teacher had any sense. Ms. Groot seemed too young, inexperienced, and lacking in wisdom to be the right person to ask.

Ms, Groot read from a prepared text provided by the state. She read with little inflection, no explanatory examples, remarks, or stories. When she thought she was being innovative, Ms. Groot projected a power point slide onto the screen and read what it said. No, Amelia thought, she wasn't going to be able to help.

Amelia Gaspe, Joe's eldest daughter, thought she was going crazy or maybe she was already crazy. She didn't just think this sometimes but walked around Muskedaigua High School seeing herself as a wild woman. Her thoughts, logical deductions, were opposed by feelings, great rushes of emotional flux, surges of disgust, fear, love. Even agony. The ordinary reactions of her fellow students convinced her she was headed for the edge.

But, it was the vividness of the dreams that she couldn't believe were happening to her. She usually dreamed powerfully at night and could not forget the content of those dreams even though she tried. In addition, daytime dream journeys were becoming unbearable and embarrassing. Except for French class and math class she would be on her dream journey mere moments after the teacher began to speak. Here was Groot intoning the reasons self-esteem was a right, and Amelia was on her dream journey almost immediately.

Amelia rose from her bed and walked to the end of the road on which her parents lived. She went towards the edge of a forest that she hadn't been allowed to enter as a child. Too dangerous. There at the woods was a beautiful, familiar, grandmotherly woman in a plain dress and moccasins waiting with an arm extended, palm up. Amelia joined her and said, "Hello Grandmother." This was her father's mother, Lucyenada, a woman Amelia had never seen but a woman she knew. "Call me Aksotha, child." They walked down paths that Lucyenada could see but Amelia just knew were there. They stopped and Amelia was instructed to look for patterns: patterns in the plants—shapes and leaves and places where they grew;, patterns in the trees—straightness, size, color, form, patterns in the light— brightness, color, intensity. Grandmother did her teaching here, using the Mohawk names for things and the ways to process them and the uses in medicine and magic. In this recurring dream, Lucyeneda taught that there was no difference between magic and medicine and mathematics, that the shapes in nature always had an underlying form that Amelia needed to discover and remember.

There were other dreams where Lucyenada took Amelia underground and terrified her or underwater and she felt her lungs fill with water. Grandmother would allow Amelia to be scared or savaged or drowned or burned or smothered nearly dead to show her that it was in her power to endure and control those things that tormented her mind and body. Aksotha convinced Amelia that her realm was all shadows. That a woman of power could see around edges and understand things others knew nothing about.

Grandmother showed her dreams of animals, fierce and frightening but helpful. She was shown her totem animal, a huge old scarred he-bear, foul-smelling and shaggy. In her dreams, the key knowledge came through the voice of the he-bear.

"Amelia Gaspe are you with us?" Ms. Groot's voice pierced the dream world.

"Not really," Amelia's reply brought titters from the girls and back-slapping belly laughs from the boys.

"I asked you to come forward and pass the graded tests back to the students and if you wouldn't mind, please stay after class for a few moments."

Amelia laid her test on her desk without looking at it. She passed out the rest as the class ended.

Any other teacher would have asked straight out, "Amelia are you taking drugs?" But Ms. Groot beat around the bush so thoroughly that Amelia never even had to deny the drug question. She had answered the drug question for the vice principal and her homeroom teacher. She wasn't unfamiliar with drugs, nor had she used them so often as to be bored. She'd gotten drunk a few times, though there was never anything left at home to try after her father had drunk his fill. Her powerful daytime dreaming was something the teachers were unprepared for. If it wasn't in their manuals, prepared by the state, it didn't exist.

Ms. Groot continued, "Your paper submitted on the control of AIDS was disappointing and showed that your failure to pay attention in class will harm your grade. One must pass health class to graduate in this state."

Amelia looked at her paper for the first time. She had been given a "D."

"What was wrong here?" She hadn't read the comments yet.

"You were not asked to develop your own theory but to explain what the government has done to control the epidemic of AIDS. You failed to do so."

"Ms. Groot, I think you are wrong. I based my paper on readings from the website of the Center for Disease Control in Atlanta. If you read the real data and skip the politically correct BS, you will find that my paper cuts through the PC veneer and…"

"Miss Gaspe, you will be required to pass health class to graduate in this state. If you continue to supply your own theories, instead of the required knowledge the state provides, you will jeopardize your graduation. Now, move on to your next class. I have another group of eager students who wish to learn." Ms. Groot put on her most stern expression and Amelia Gaspe realized again that an education and learning were separate and oftentimes opposite endeavors.

Chapter 7

June 23rd

M el Dumke is an odd-looking and ugly man. Viewed from any angle, his head appears to be an upside down pyramid. From front or back, the top is flat and from the sides, the back appears flat. This effect exaggerates his nose and makes him always seem to be looming toward anyone near him.

He personifies Melvin Loonch's description of the clientele at the Musky County Fair: "Ugly white people in bad clothes." He was driving a navy blue short bus his employer had purchased at the auto auction. He drove parallel to the Harborway, the elevated highway that enters Pantherville from the southern lakeshore suburbs. One must drive south off the Harborway and travel in front of several defunct industrial properties before turning back to reach the sailboat marinas, arrayed in sequence along the inner harbor.

Some of these industrial properties have officially become nature preserves, but they are all semi-urban wildlife sanctuaries. They've grown up into the scrubby bushes and trees so beloved of deer, raccoons, skunks, and wild turkeys. The road goes straight south for several miles with an occasional branch to the left that loops under the

Harborway and heads back north. A wrong choice of when to turn under the elevated highway can cause one to have to repeat a different concentric loop.

The road ends where the last marina or yacht brokerage is on the inner harbor side and the Coast Guard station complex is on the outer harbor side. Dumke got there and knew he'd gone too far— his "fare'" was to be at the second to last marina, Bog's Yachts, which he'd passed without noticing. Forced to turn under the highway and run back south three miles before starting another loop, he cursed three times and picked up his speed. Dumke only got paid for delivering his fares. Failed attempts didn't pay off. Putting diesel fuel in a short bus wasn't cheap (his only expense was fuel) and he couldn't afford the cost of missing a pick-up. He'd be late, but he'd still try.

To add to his frustration, he aborted the second loop when he saw the two police cars, with lights flashing, three all-white Chevy Suburbans, and other official cars loom behind him and speed past, headed north. Mel pulled over and bit his lower lip. The night sky at the marina was lit up with the flashing blue lights of emergency boats; he turned back under the highway and headed south to safety. He'd lost fifty dollars per rag head for eight camel jockeys; four hundred dollars left lying on the table. Mel Dumke needed a beer.

"Stop here, I'll go have a look." Moses X. Snow was ready to go searching for the invaders, as he called all illegal immigrants floating over to Pantherville from Ontario.

Rad stopped the Malibu, though she couldn't see anything "here" that was different than the coarse scrubby brush all along this endless loop of a road.

"Just keep going around the loop until you see this," he held up his red neckerchief, "tied to a bush. That will be me." Rad cruised the loop at the legal speed thinking about what she'd gotten into with this latest escapade of Joe Gaspe's.

Radleigh Loonch didn't know Mo Snow; she'd only met him briefly at Jackie B's, and didn't know what to make of him as they'd raced along in the Malibu, sent on a mission by Joe Gaspe. Mo spoke in that familiar Canadian accent so reminiscent of the commentators on Hockey Night in Canada. At the same time he had a little bit of the French Canadian accent and something else that almost sounded like Russian or Greek or Hungarian. She couldn't figure out why he was along on this mission except that he was Joe's cousin and would do anything for him.

Moses X Snow was from Kahnawake, the compound of the Onkwehonwe, the Real people, near Montreal, which partially explained his French tilted Canadian English. Mo was a Mohawk, he considered himself to be a person of his tribe's separate country, but as a practical man he realized that he was also a citizen of two modern countries, Canada and the USA. His unique access to all the cultures of the area—two kinds of Canadians, six tribes of Haudenosonee (people of the longhouse), more actually, if you count the Hurons, Mohicans, Abenaki and others, and American—made him a man of so many worlds as to have access to anything anywhere.

Mohawks officially live in Ontario, Quebec, and New York State, with their own nation divided into several reservations. They are a nation that has fought against itself in three wars: the, so-called French and Indian wars, the most well known of which was the Seven Years War, that ended in 1763, the American Revolution, and the war of 1812. From a white man's perspective they were winners and losers in all these wars. From a Mohawk perspective, they were only losers. However, the Mohawks saw their historical role, as the brokers of union in the Iroquois league, being reprised by bringing the USA and Canada together, while reuniting their nation.

Like many Mohawks, Mo Snow had worked in the high steel, building skyscrapers in New York City, Toronto and other eastern cities. Mohawks showed no fear walking the girders of skyscrapers. Unfortunately, some individual Mohawks were enticed by the raven and the white man's intoxicating drinks, WPLJ and Muscatel. Those beverages had sent Real People flying to their deaths. Mo Snow had been one of the fifty Mohawks who showed up to help work the steel at Ground Zero right after the attack. That was before the official first responders took over.

On the second loop, Rad caught a glimpse of a familiar-looking navy blue short bus as it turned three fourths of a mile ahead. She recognized it as the vehicle that had nearly hit Joe on the return trip from the Oil Seep Rez.

Rad thought back to that day as she drove. When they had gotten back in the Malibu after the excitement of Joe's near miss died down—the car had suffered a dent in the hood made by Joe's ample butt—she'd said. "That was no accident Joe, that bus tried to run you down."

"No kidding, did you get a look at the driver?"

"Uh-unh."

"It seems someone doesn't want us looking into the Derek Chang murder."

"Did you see anything, Joe?"

"I may have recognized someone's face. I'll tell you in a few days after I have dreamed on it."

"Okay…" Rad let that last syllable just lie there, like a modern college girl does, as if to say, "I can't believe that you believe anything so lame."

"Why are you doing this unofficial sleuthing, Joe? You're not a cop or FBI or anything. Why risk your life when you're not a professional?"

"Did you see what was done to us on September Eleventh?"

"Don't patronize me, Joe!" Rad snapped. "I was as moved by that as anyone."

"Alright, I'm sorry. I guess I want to do something that isn't a waste of time or an absolute failure."

"Whattaya mean?"

"I'm over forty years old," Joe was looking straight ahead but his eyes were unfocused and he was speaking in a bland voice without inflection. Rad glanced at him as she drove. He appeared to be giving a recitation of a speech he had memorized but never delivered. "I'm a bit of a drunk. I flit from job to job. I haven't got a decent car or a valid driver's license. I get in trouble a lot; little stuff but it's embarrassing. I think my wife hates me. I keep sinking money into custom fishing rods no one can afford to buy. More than anything, though, I have five daughters and I don't hardly know any of them. My oldest is probably completely lost to me, but I may have a chance with the other four. I want to do something I can be proud of to prove to my daughters that I am somebody."

"Your wife doesn't hate you. You already are somebody, a great guy, well liked. Anyway, what you're doing now, besides being dangerous, is secret. Even when you succeed you'll not be able to tell the girls."

"The change will be in me. They'll know through their dreaming. My oldest inherited the woman's power to dream from my mother, her grandmother, but she has had no one to help her along the path to power."

"That's the second time you've mentioned dreams. What is this dreaming stuff?"

Joe snapped out of his trance and pointed at the sky, "A dream is destiny revealed." A red-tailed hawk crossed the road just in front of Rad's Malibu.

Rad was worried now: it was her fourth loop, she had seen an enemy of Joe's driving a navy blue short bus, Mo had not returned, and she was convinced that the driver of the bus had seen her Malibu—there were hundreds of metallic sandstone-painted Malibus and she'd had the dent removed from her hood, but still... Then she saw the red flag ahead. She pulled to a stop. There were no cars behind and nothing visible ahead. Rad looked into the brambles and Mo stepped out, retrieved his neckerchief and slipped into the passenger seat.

"We can leave. Everything is okay. You might want to call Marv's cell phone so Joe knows, mission accomplished."

"What the heck was the mission?" Rad got exasperated when she didn't know what was going on. This whole thing of shadowing Joe and his network was frustrating her.

"I went down the path there to see if the Border Patrol had picked up those Arabs sneaking into the country next to the grain elevators. That was a path for one of the Real People, nettles, brambles, blackberry canes, rose bushes; you'd have hated it. But at the water's edge I could see the patrol boats all lit up with their blue lights surrounding a sailboat. I was watching when that little black fellow—the FBI guy; came up to me...."

"Mo, agent Andre is an African-American, black is no longer the accepted term."

"Right, well that little black guy moved through the brush as silently as a Mohawk and came up to me and told me that the invaders had been captured by the Coast Guard and would be processed by the Border Patrol. Funny thing, that little guy didn't have a smudge on his clothes, hadn't been snagged by a thorn, hadn't broken a sweat, he looked like he was in an air-conditioned office. Maybe he is one of the Real People."

"So, Joe warned them about these guys and they were captured?"

"Yes, eh? Though your agent said he thought immigration would just send them back over the bridge to try again."

Chapter 8

July 4th

The closing of the Straits one-half hour before dark on Independence Day was a tradition born of necessity. So many boats had cracked up because of distracted drivers that it had become too dangerous to leave the situation unaddressed. There were the boats full of families drifting the river, ready to watch as town after town displayed its fireworks. Also, there were drifting boats full of revelers drunk from a day's exertions bending elbows. Then there were those that decided to run from display to display. When the runners were also the revelers, weaving through drifting boats, collisions occurred.

The policy was not really fair to the Canadian boaters wanting to use the waterway. But Canadians also enjoyed American spectacles, fireworks and football being two. Though displeased, they were accustomed to being shouldered aside by their big brother across the river.

Joe Gaspe was at Royal Marina with his wife and four of his five girls on the holiday, using his binoculars to watch the straits. He watched for crosscurrent traffic as the night deepened to full dark. He had gotten a hint from Mel Dumke that there would be an attempt to exploit the confusion and the diverted attention during the first hour of full darkness. A large number of boats would be returning to the launch sites and marinas after the several fireworks displays had died down, usually between ten PM and ten-thirty. It would be impossible for the watchers from Homeland Security to notice everything.

"A bunch of Niggerauguans are coming over and I've gotta drive the beaneaters to Jimmy town." Mel Dumke had been complaining to a few of the older fishermen hanging around Jackie B's. Joe had been informed of these remarks and had alerted the authorities. Everyone was out; the Border Patrol had boats on the river and watchers on the shore, the Coast Guard had two boats on patrol, the County Sheriff's boat was moving from boat to boat, greeting and profiling as they went. Joe Gaspe was only one man but he had a feeling, gleaned from eavesdropping on Mel Dumke, that the Red Rock Lock was where the immigrants were going to land. The breakwall outside the lock, a favorite spot for shore fishermen and summertime squatters, was lined with people for the fireworks displays of Saturday night, July 4th.

It would be a simple matter, if they got ashore, for the Nicaraguans to walk out across the access road beside the railroad bridge and disperse from Straits Avenue into the night. They could hop on a bus, walk away, or get picked up by an accomplice, which seemed to be Dumke's assignment.

While Kate and his daughters watched the sky, Joe scanned the Canadian shore looking for a boat on the move. Boats were bobbing up and down, some using their running lights: green and red in front, white on top and in the back; some using their anchor lights, white only on top. The flashes from cigarette lighters as the smokers lit up, or a spotlight as someone searched for an item in their boat, added a strobic effect to the scene. All these lights were reflected and sent shimmering across the straits by the waves and the bobbing of boats on the water.

Joe was getting a headache from the effort of concentration combined with one of those nasty hangovers caused by drinking early, stopping, and then staying awake. He rubbed his temples and looked upstream toward a small boat launch situated above Frog Creek on the

Ontario side. He had concluded that it was from this launch the boat would drift down on the Red Rock Lock breakwall, using small silent bursts of power from an electric trolling motor. Then the immigrants could scrabble up on the wall and ooh and ah with those watching the exploding shells from the towns along the straits.

"You know that you're an immigrant too, don't you, Joe Gaspe." This was the voice of his wood shop teacher, the man who had taught him to paint and work with wood. Those four years in wood shop, as student and then student instructor, had enabled Joe to endure high school. Never an academic, Joe was a girl chaser and a scrapper. When he wasn't in trouble it was only because he'd gotten away with some mischief. The mentoring of Mr. Ray was part of his development as a man.

Here was Mr. Ray invading his dreams to tell him what a mutt he was. Joe was the seventh son of an Irish father and a Mohawk mother. However, Joe had been brought up in the home of his mother's sister and her Quebecois husband. They adopted Joe and two of his brothers after his parents had died in an auto accident. The necessity for several families to adopt the seven wild boys caused him to be raised with only two of his six brothers.

Joe's ancestry was more mixed than anyone was likely to believe. Consequently, he was of two minds about the part of his job that entailed reporting on illegal aliens. He knew from briefings by the Border Patrol that Canada leaked illegal immigrants into the US like a sieve. There were essentially three categories of these migrants. There were economic refugees trying for a better life in America and a chance for their descendants to become official Americans. There were hundreds of Chinese migrants, refugees from the Communist takeover of Hong Kong, able to get into Canada because of British Commonwealth ties between Hong Kong and Canada. The Chinese were also smuggled in trailer-loads by big-time immigrant brokers who charged them everything they had to be stuffed into a ship and snuck into the western coast of Canada. These people were often in fearfully rough shape by the time they were ferried across the Musky

Straits into the United States. Mixed in with these economic refugees were a generous helping of agents of the People's Liberation Army who were coming to facilitate the movement and prospective mayhem of the last group, the smallest and most dangerous.

That third group comprised the Islamic terrorists bent on the destruction and defeat of the West. Driven by ideology and fanaticism, they didn't realize or care that they were tools of the Chinese Communist leadership.

Joe's dreams kept bringing him back to the economic group, especially the Latin Americans. He saw them cutting grass, slinging hash, and cleaning offices. They were saving money so their children could have a start in the USA. Joe never felt good about turning these folks in and never felt bad when he missed a few.

He dreamt badly whenever he told his bosses about a family or two of Hispanics seeking the better life.

A Mohawk attaches so much importance to his power dreaming that Joe would suffer both mentally and physically for days when he dreamed badly.

Jackie B was also on the breakwall at the end of the lock. He had several of his nets out and his two helpers were dipping minnows off the end of the wall. As the current of the straits passed the wall, it curled back into the slack water of the Royal Marina and the discharge basin of the Red Rock Lock. The hydraulic forces of the backwash caused a permanent eddy to exist off the end of the breakwall. The eddy held baitfish (minnows) at all times of the year. Licensed bait dealers, dipping emerald shiners off the end of the wall, were a completely ordinary sight. Even though it was the dark of night on the fourth of July, Jackie B's crew drew no attention.

While his crew did the work, Jackie wandered back along the wall towards where Joe had told him the contraband smugglers had been dropping their cargo. It was a simple matter for them to scramble up onto the wall and walk out to Straits Avenue where the bus stopped. That started a journey that would take them anywhere in the United States. If one carried a fishing pole and a bucket, he looked like he was just a shore angler returning from fishing. Joe had recruited a street kid named Julio who told him that he and his friends had been recovering cheap fishing poles and empty pails from an abandoned restaurant near the bus stop, on a regular basis.

Jackie felt a small tinge of guilt as he noted the many Styrofoam bait cups that fisherman had dropped along the shore. Such slobs they were, and posing as nature lovers, too. He regretted the day Styrofoam had replaced cardboard. Rain and sun would rot cardboard away. The only hope for Styrofoam is that it would eventually be broken into bits. The overwhelming amount of garbage left Jackie unsure as to where the illegals had been coming ashore. He found a hidey-hole in the rocks, where he could watch any heads that might come up above the wall, because they would be silhouetted against the horizon and the cityscape of Pantherville. Jackie watched while his crew worked and the crowd concentrated on the fireworks displays.

Radleigh Loonch

Chapter 9

July 7

The Independent Order of Odd Fellows (IOOF) hall was the scene for the monthly meetings of the Straits Musky Club. It consisted of two rooms, thirty by sixty feet. One was a meeting hall and one was a barroom. As the meeting time approached, the barroom was crowded with those ordering their drinks and chicken wings. Slowly they would spill into the meeting room for talk of muskies caught and hot follows—musky fishing is a sport where almost-caught fish, followers, get nearly as much play in the lore as those actually boated—as well as club business, raffles, occasional guest speakers, and good cheer.

Joe Gaspe had set himself up at a round table in the bar with his three interns where he could smoke and hold court with his friends and admirers. He had a Labatt's Blue in front of him and his twenty wings were on order. Ger Blog, and Kyle Buchhalter sat to his left and Rad Loonch was on his right. An attractive young woman was always a sensation at a meeting dominated by men and Rad drew her share of admirers and inspectors to the table. They talked to Joe while looking over Rad. She was dressed casually, but conservatively. That didn't inhibit the men from checking her out.

Rad was reminded of a new trend that she had heard of called speed dating. A number of women sat at desks and conducted five-minute interviews with men who might be potential dates. It was similar to exchanging business cards but more interactive and designed to eliminate all the non-starters. Joe was conducting speed interviews. He had told Rad that five or six musky anglers were all he needed to round out his network.

Ned Niawanda, successful musky troller, warehouseman, and a man who worked the harbor but not the Straits was rejected. "Too sure of himself, doesn't spend enough time in the river. He's my good friend." Joe said.

Johnny Lawrence, charter captain, dedicated fisherman, a man who got around, was accepted.

"You wanna pay back those guys who did 9-11 to us?" asked Gaspe.

"Damn straight." Lawrence was pumped.

"You ready and willing to keep your eyes open in the river and the lake? Report anything suspicious, keep the proper authorities informed?"

"Whatever it takes."

Joe handed him a plain white business card. It read:

Thomas Andre,
Special Projects,
Department of Homeland Security

"This gentleman will contact you for an interview; don't call him, he'll call you. If you're in, he'll let you know. Take it from me, partner, you're part of the team." Joe moved on to the next interview.

In rapid succession he accepted: Jason "Kid" Kohl, up-and-coming river caster and lure manufacturer; John Johns, lure maker, deli king, and madman who knew everyone; Tom Booker, expert troller and man of the river; and Melvin Loonch, Radleigh's father, philosopher, iconoclast and genuine pain in the rear. In accepting Rad's Dad into the network Joe commented in an aside to Rad, "He's nuts, but hey, he's one of my partners."

Joe rejected some potential net members. With Marty Aud, the interview went differently.

"You wanna pay back those guys for 9-11?"

"I despise George Bush."

"You ready and willing…?"

"I despise George Bush," he interrupted.

"OK, thanks good buddy, I'll talk to you later." Aside to Rad, he muttered, "Helluva a fisherman, but not right for this."

Rad was beginning to understand how Joe Gaspe broke down his acquaintances as: cousins-those very close to him; partners—friends whose peccadilloes he could overlook; good friends—those who were okay, but not right for him; and good buddies—people he didn't really like.

Joe turned to Rad, ignoring Ger Blog and Kyle Buckhalter as they tucked in to their beer and chicken wings, and said, "With Slim Tomkins, and Magnus Markson on the team, as well as all these guys, we'll be covering the water until the end of November for my partner Agent Andre."

The musky club meeting crowd was long gone and Joe was the only guy left at the bar. He liked the IOOF hall since, as a private club, smoking was still allowed. The nanny state government was in the process of banning everything, or so Joe thought.

"They're gonna ban smoking in cars, just you wait," the bartender had a cigarette going, too.

"How can they do that? It's like my house! As a member of the longhouse, tobacco is a sacred herb of our religion."

"I hate the government of Jew York, bastards cut off my unemployment illegally," Joe recognized that bitter voice behind him, and turned around to see that Mel Dumke had entered the bar.

"Hey, Mel, let me set you up. What'll you have?"

"Bud." The bartender brought one and a Blue for Joe. He took the required money from the bills sitting in front of Joe and retreated to the other end of the bar. Dumke leaned on the bar next to Joe.

"You staying in town?"

"Yeah, I got abandoned, I think. My partner, Marv, cut a trail back to Muskedaigua. I left the club meeting to see a guy's new Harley. When I got back Marv thought I'd left and he'd split."

"All those musky club pricks are gone?" Mel Dumke had unspecified beefs with a lot of people and groups; Joe began to remember that as one of the reasons he grew annoying. But duty called.

"I'm the only musky man left. What are you up to?"

"You're the only one I can stand. I've got a little errand to do, want to come along? There might be some broads involved at the end. Besides I can put you up for the night on my couch if you want."

Joe knew, or thought he knew, that this man had tried to run him down in Dover Corners. He was pretty sure that Dumke was behind the dumping of Derek Chang's body. He had been told Dumke was an operative for those he was pursuing. He imagined a raven descending on each shoulder, one was danger and one was opportunity. Joe had his Irish father's capacity for drinking but also had his Mohawk mother's weakness for firewater. He was not a man of judgment when he had a snootful. He went for the ride. He didn't figure to spend the night and had seen the kind of women attracted to Mel Dumke, but he had to see about this errand.

The van they climbed into was red and had a landscaping logo on the side that, Joe saw when he walked around to the passenger's side, said, "*Spring Peeper's Lawn and Garden Keepers,*" with a stylized frog above it. Joe got in, hoping to find out whether this was the van that took Chang on his last ride, and whether he was in bigger trouble than he thought.

Joe was a smoker but his grandmother, stepmother, and mother had been Mohawks, so he knew how to sort out smells. The odors present in Mel Dumke's van were a puzzle that Joe solved directly. First he had to disregard Dumke's body odor, a sour vinegary smell, poorly covered by a heavy spackling of cologne. Then there were the work smells of a landscape van, gasoline, fertilizer, weed killer, and strongly present between the bucket seats, was the pesticide Sevin. Joe looked in the back and saw a tarp lying in a corner. He looked at the road and saw them approaching the Big Island bridge tollbooth. He tried to hand Mel the 75-cent toll.

"Don't need it. I've got Easy Pass."

"My partner, Mel Loonch, calls that Easy Fleece, heh heh heh." Joe turned to the back again as he said that, looked at the tarp, and caught the odor that he had wondered about. It was there, lurking under those stronger smells, blood, urine, feces, death. This was the van of Derek Chang's last ride.

Joe turned to face forward and Mel said, "We had to clean up a road kill deer last week, right in a customer's driveway. You know how these rich bitches are, too good to clean up their own yards, and too squeamish to look at dead animals. We couldn't even put it in with the trash and it was garbage day," Dumke took his thumb and pushed up the end of his nose with it.

Mohawks can smell deer scat from a mile away. Deer don't eat Chinese cabbage, at least not after it is cooked.

As they crossed the Musky Straits on the bridge, Joe looked into the dark water and thought about those muskies down there waiting for a fisherman like him. This was a location that he fished with Marv often and they seldom saw anyone other than Melvin Loonch fishing there.

Dumke took the second exit, turned right, went half a mile, then turned left, went a few hundred yards, then right and pulled into a driveway next to a white van.

"We're gonna switch cars here." Despite the late hour the house had its garage light on and a female figure was standing in the kitchen doorway. Joe stood by the car and lit up a generic filter cigarette. Mel went to the door and spoke to the woman, looming large in her housecoat, through the half-open door. He got the keys, opened the white van; and told Joe to hop in.

"What's this errand, old buddy?" Joe was glad to be out of the van that smelled like a dead person, but he was nervous about what might happen next. He had been in several fistfights in his younger days and considered himself to be pretty fair hand in a fight. He carried a folding Buck knife, but Dumke or one of his associates might have a gun.

"You've come this far, let's see it through," he thought.

"We're going to pick up some people. I get $50 a head." There was a cloth curtain hung behind the bucket seats of this van and when Joe parted it he saw a board bench along each side.

"Close that." Dumke said. Joe complied.

"We're going to travel this road," he indicated West Straits Drive, "three times. When we see a pile of rocks, three high, we're going to stop and pick up some gooks."

"These are illegals?"

"Why do you think that every small town in America now has two Chinese restaurants? I hate that Jap Crap, but if these slopes wanna come over here and get screwed by our country and I can make some bucks "fa-sill-it-tatin'" that, I'll take the money. You should get in on this, Joe—there's no end to these rice eaters and the money is cash per head. When we get back I'll take you to meet the big boss, so you can sign up."

"I don't know."

It worked out just as Dumke said, there were two piles of three rocks. On the third pass, he stopped the van, pressed the unlock button, and a small squad of Asian men and women came from the woods and silently piled into the back of the van. After the second group had been picked up, the van was crammed full. They were all young adults, no children, no old people.

The trip back to the landscaping van was designed to lose anyone who might be tailing them. It was almost three AM when they pulled into the driveway. The light in the driveway went out. A Mercedes sedan pulled in behind the van full of immigrants and two big men got out. Dumke clicked open the door and said to Joe, "You should get out and go into the carport straight ahead." Joe did so.

One man opened the van and counted heads, the other counted out bills. The men were in business suits despite the hour: they were Asian, but of an entirely different body shape than the slight ones in the van. These men were not as big as Sumo wrestlers but they were thick and square and their suit coats bulged beneath the arms. They could have been twins. Or clones. One handed Dumke the bills and got in the Mercedes and it drove away. One got behind the wheel in the white van and drove away. Mel Dumke came into the carport, joined Joe and said, "A thousand dollars for, what? Three hours work?" he handed Joe a fifty dollar bill. It was crisp and slippery. Joe carefully slipped it into his shirt pocket.

"Thanks. I didn't do much." Joe felt guilty, but he thought Agent Andre might want to look at the bill.

"Come on in and meet my lady friend," By going through the carport, they went into a kitchen that smelled of coffee and cinnamon buns.

Mel's lady friend was a woman of considerable size with black dyed hair and white pancake makeup. This created quite a contrast in the Fluorescent kitchen lighting. She looked like a TV actress mingling with the audience. She was not an attractive woman, jowly, and with a wide forehead. She had the down-turned mouth of someone perpetually pissed off. This was always a mystery to Joe, and probably most men: if you're ugly, why be mean about it, how's that going to help? She acknowledged Joe's presence in the way that a woman has of honing in on a prey species. Joe was a mark for her to tell about herself, her favorite and perpetual subject.

"I'm Lorraine Czeck, that's pronounced sack, and Mel and I've been together for sixteen months." (This name stunned Joe, as it was the maiden name of his Gypsy grandmother). "I'm a teacher in the Big Island school district and I'm emptying those heads full of mush every day. Teaching these little spoiled brats how bad things really are in this country, with men in charge of such polluting, exploiting, big businesses like those that have taken advantage of Mel. He tells me you've been laid off and had it rough, too. Well, Joe, give us teachers a few more years and we'll have people ready to take over this country, if we can get them away from their parents' influence. I've already got a couple of poor little rich girls, all compassion and feeling, working for us; they open their boathouses on the Gold Coast so the immigrants can land unseen and work their way to their rendezvous in the woods. These girls have high powered fathers and mothers, the type of never-home, give 'em money, rich bastards who've ruined this country…"

She rattled on, giving Joe the feeling that a nail-gun was snapping ten-penny sinkers right into his frontal lobe. Dumke, who had perfected the talent of not listening at all, was tucked into his third cinnamon bun and slurping away at his coffee.

Seizing a chance to get away, Joe said, "I'm going out for a smoke, I'll be by the van."

"Wait Joe, let me call my boss. I'll see if he wants to let you in on the action. Let me make that call." Mel was dialing as Joe went outside.

Joe took his chance to avoid his last ride. He went out the carport door and walked to his left, hopped a fence, doubled back through a side yard, and sprinted for ten seconds, then settled into a loping gait that he'd perfected when hunting with his stepfather that enabled him to run long distances without getting winded, despite his pack-a-day cigarette habit.

The last sound he heard was the car door slamming just after Mel Dumke called out his name. Joe was headed for Otter Creek State Park, a place that he had scoped out during the Straits Musky Club picnic.

Rad got a call on her cell phone the next morning before she left on her morning drive to Muskedaigua. It was Joe. He told her to pick him up on Big Island instead of the Park and Ride where they usually met. Afterward, they joined Agent Andre at a Greek restaurant.

During breakfast Rad pressed Agent Andre as to why Mel Dumke was running free after, she was certain, he had tried to murder Joe Gaspe.

"Is he somebody's brother-in-law or has he got pictures of somebody? Why not take him down?" She was concerned for her own safety, but more so for a man she'd come to worry about, Joe Gaspe.

"The Department of Homeland Security is not vulnerable to cheap blackmail." Thomas Andre was a man whose gentle demeanor and open face made him seem very affable, but no one climbed through a bureaucracy, like the FBI, without some streak of iron ore in his fiber. It was this that Rad saw in the agent's flashing eyes. She had pushed too hard, and the look he gave her was serious and frightening.

"Is he CIA?" Joe interrupted to take the heat off of Rad.

Andre turned sharply to Joe and said, "I do not know of any CIA agents operating undercover within the United States. Domestic surveillance is under the jurisdiction of the Department of Justice."

Joe noted that this was bureau-speak for neither yes nor no. He used a paper napkin to remove the crisp fifty-dollar bill from his shirt pocket.

"Maybe you can get a lift off this or trace the serial number. Dumke gave it to me for driving around with him this morning. He claims to want me on his team—I disappeared before his handlers came back to meet me."

"We'll see what we can do." Andre didn't press Joe for details. "Someone will contact you if we find anything you need to know."

When they had first started working together, Joe Gaspe offered himself as a sexual partner to Radleigh Loonch. She was driving to a meeting with Jackie B. She laughed at him and said, "In your dreams, old man."

"I don't mean to offend you but when I meet a woman, I ask right away if she wants to fool around. If not, I'm okay with that and if so, I'm okay with that too."

"You actually get some women to accept that proposal?"

"More than you'd think."

"Well yeah, cause I wouldn't think it would be any."

"Why? Is there something wrong with me?" Joe raised his elbow and took a sniff of his armpit.

"Joe, I'm sure you're fine, for an old guy, but you don't understand what women want."

"Maybe all women don't want the same things."

Neither spoke for a while though neither was truly offended. Joe kept thinking about that "in your dreams" comment. He hadn't decided yet how to explain to Rad the power of the dreaming engaged in by Mohawks.

He dreamt that night in the old way and woke to quickly write down what he'd dreamed.

Joe, in the doorway of a tall wooden building of at least five stories, was looking straight up and couldn't see the top. A woman, not Rad, an older mature woman who exuded sexuality, was at the top of a flight of stairs. She beckoned him. He charged up the stairs taking two at a time, breathing easily, like a hunter trailing a wounded deer.

At the top of the stairs Joe ran right into a shining pool. All was brightness as he plunged, surfaced, and shook his head, spraying droplets from his hair. The woman pulled him from the water. She was instantly at the top of another set of stairs.

These were steeper. Joe took them one at a time and began to feel the effects of the work he was doing. He reached the top and dove into a new pool, duller, grayer, with slightly stained water, He felt pressure on his head and ears as he plunged and rose. He shook his head, and water plopped off into the pool. The goddess/woman hugged him and wrestled him through the door.

Now she was at the top of a third set of stairs. These were very steep, the risers were so high he had to summon the strength to jump and grab a handhold for every one. Building energy and expending it, he struggled his way almost straight up. He slid into a dark pool at the top, water the color of strong tea. Bubbles escaped from his lips and he felt pressure on his head as if it were in a vise. He surfaced and she was sitting poolside, radiant, and shining against the night sky. He crawled from the pool and was barely able to stand.

He looked up the face of a cliff and she looked down over the top, a white aura surrounding her head. He leaned so far back to look at her that he fell backward into the pool that was now as black as dark beer. Air bubbles escaped his mouth, the pressure on his head increased, a second set of bubbles was let go and the pressure was yet more intense. Joe felt like sinking. Then he felt his arms being draped over the back of the shining woman and she brought him to poolside.

Joe sat, too weak to rise; he was happy but in a cloud of fog, unable to see. The only clear thing in his vision was a branch of the herb bittersweet, pointing downward with its orange berries attached. She lay down beside him. He laid back and they slid into the pool. It was inky black. Bubbles escaped from his mouth, pressure built on his head, and she lifted him for a breath. She pulled him down, bubbles escaped, pressure built, she lifted him for a breath. She pulled him down, bubbles escaped, pressure built, she lifted him for air. He floated to the shallow end of the pool and saw her lips shape the words, thank you. She faded with the dawn light until she became transparent and then invisible.

Chapter 10

July 14th

With the summer in full bloom, the Wednesday night sailboat races were a thing of beauty. They were an example of all that was right about the Pantherville region. All the boats were out, the expensive ones, the crummy ones, the big ones, the barely-there ones, the beautiful ones—there was an encouraging percentage of stunning boats. Every way that men could compete was displayed on Wednesday. They competed by being the fastest. They competed by being the most skilled sailors. They competed by being the most expensive and by being the cheapest. They competed by making a statement of their sophistication and by making an anti-statement of their lack of sophistication. They competed by being the biggest and by being the dinkiest. They competed by being the newest and by being the oldest. They competed by being the most modern and the most primitive.

Joe had picked up a tip at Jackie B's by sitting, and listening, and drinking, and smoking, that someone was going to move some Chinese migrants right under the nose of the Coast Guard. Joe was out with Rad, in waves of a size that he would normally decline, to check out whether his source, a Japanese-American salmon fisherman called Jeff Sagamaka, was reliable. Before she began to feel the waves Rad had been marveling to herself how much of Joe's information came to him without him doing much of anything.

Sometimes they would go "on maneuvers," as Joe put it, to talk with people, but mostly Joe hung out in the barroom at Jackie B's, drank beer, and listened to fishermen talk. Folks wasted a lot of time and burned a lot of gasoline flying around the country. The thing to do, Joe said, "Was to set up shop somewhere with provisions—Jackie B's had beer and allowed smoking—and keep your eyes and ears open. Only ask questions when you have to. Most people loved to talk about their favorite subject, themselves. Just get them started and wait. They'd tell you everything they had done, believed they had done, or planned to do, eventually."

Whoever was advising these sets of water-borne migrants was giving them one bum steer after another. Joe wondered whether it was Mel Dumke playing a double game or Mel Dumke being a screw-up. If Dumke was playing a double game and actually working for the government then... no, Dumke's hate of the government and all authority was genuine. And besides, he'd been involved in the death of Derek Chang and tried twice to kill Joe as well.

It must be one screw-up after another. Here came another incongruous sight that had to be a Dumke cock-up. Maybe it was a language problem. The Wednesday open sailboat races were much bigger than the ones on Tuesday nights, as both men and women pilots and captains were included. The harbor was loaded with boats of several classes. Because of the waves, many of the less adept sailors had not made it past the breakwalls.

There was plenty of wind this evening and the five-foot swells were occasionally doubling up and pounding over the top of the breakwalls. Joe was staying inside the walls for two reasons. It was difficult to fish out there among the rollers and Rad was seasick. Having already spewed chunks overboard, she was dry-retching spittle, and moaning as she lolled over the port side of the Whaler.

The rough seas made the putt-putting plywood rowboat even more unbelievable. Joe had noticed it when it was a mile outside the harbor. It disappeared from view when it entered a wave trough and came into view on the wave tops. Now that it had gotten some shelter behind the lighthouse wall, Joe saw that it was overcrowded, unseaworthy, and had two men bailing as fast as they could with coffee cans. The sailors were busy working their boats, dealing with the wind and waves, but many took a good look at the ridiculous overloaded plywood twelve-footer. Joe dialed up from channel nine to channel sixteen, on the marine band radio, to listen to any one talking to the Coast Guard.

The emergency channel was a cacophony of calls from sailboats telling the Coasties about this boat that obviously did not belong in the middle of the Wednesday races. The Coast Guard Patrol Boat showed up while Joe watched. They had trouble tying onto the smaller boat, since it did not even have a rope onboard. The Coast Guard boat managed to get a crewman on board the sinking skiff. He timed the rise of the swells and boosted people into the Patrol Boat one at a time. Though no longer taking water over the side, the rowboat was leaking seriously. When those bailing stopped, the plywood craft sank rapidly. The last few occupants and the rescuer went into the water in life jackets as the boat sank from view. The meager possessions of the immigrants floated away.

Joe's network had warned him to look for this attempt but it was so lame that he didn't need to do anything about it. It was time to take Rad, who had turned a sickly greenish color, had her eyes closed, and her hair plastered to her head, back to land.

Sam Hung was waiting in the Ford stretch van. He had borrowed it from the Unitarian Church telling them that he needed to help his cousin move. They asked no questions. He was parked at R&R yachts to pick up the immigrants. He was to transfer them to Mel Dumke, waiting with his blue bus in the parking lot of a closed-down waterfront restaurant. It was part of the plan that a speaker of Mandarin was required to reassure the people, since they would be scared and suspicious of any barbarian. Sam didn't like this work but the person with power over his mother had required it and he was compelled to do as arranged.

A call came through on his cell phone. He connected without speaking.

"Singapore Sling," the caller disconnected. This meant things had gone wrong and Sam started the van and headed under the Harborway and went a half-mile before turning into the restaurant parking lot.

Mel Dumke was sitting in a lawn chair in front of his blue short bus. He was fishing from the bank though the line in the water had no bait on it.

The white van was the one he expected, but it was early. He looked up as Lucky Hung slammed on the brakes and threw up a spray of gravel. Instead of unloading passengers, he shook his head, floored the gas pedal, and did a tire-squealing one hundred-eighty degree turn. Going out the way he had come, he sprayed a lot more gravel in a perfect arc as he left.

Dumke reeled in his rod, gathered his lawn chair and his adult beverage, and boarded the blue bus. Another pickup gone wrong, the bosses were going to be pissed and he wasn't going to be paid. Cursing to himself, Dumke headed for home.

The two silver Franklin half-dollars had grown to three-inch discs in Joe's dreaming but the reason for their brief recurrence in his dreams was still a mystery. In trying to re-dream them he had seen that the mystery participant was in fact Mo Snow and Gaspe wanted to remember to ask Mo about that. That dream fragment was still stuck when Joe saw himself on the Musky Straits in his Boston Whaler. *He was going north, up the Straits, and was being squeezed by two boats. It was a busy summer Sunday. The combined boat wakes of the traffic bounced off the wall on the American side and, amplified in the necked down aspect of that stretch of water, had caused three-foot waves. Joe's boat had nowhere to go, a thirty-two foot Coastliner was lumbering along, overtaking him from the starboard side. He should be able to outrun a boat with that much drag but the Whaler wasn't responding. He advanced the throttles and the boat missed and sputtered as if only one outboard was pulling.*

Roaring up on his port side and squeezing him as well, was a twenty-one-foot Coastliner. He couldn't outrun this boat either. He was buffeted from each side. Each boat had a driver, shrouded in black; only the pilot's black eyes were visible to Joe. They were glaring at him, as they steered into him. This action took place between the Friendship Bridge and the Railroad Bridge, probably in Canadian waters, or close to it. There was someone on Joe's boat, cursing and shouting, but Joe didn't turn to see who it was, his eyes were on the water ahead. The port side boat closed the six-inch gap and smacked into him, forcing him into the starboard side boat that would gun its engine, and push him back into the port side boat. These maneuvers kept rocking him, left, then right, then back again. The yelling continued getting louder.

Suddenly, the boat to the right burst into flames, smoke billowing from the cabin. Joe slammed his throttle into neutral. He would drop back. But the boats were locked together. He tried reverse. He couldn't move back because his boat was stuck fast to the larger starboard side boat. Serpent-tongued flames were licking toward Joe's Whaler.

Then, the boat on the port side became involved in the fire as well. Joe saw that he was going to be consumed by fire if he stayed with the Whaler. He ran to the stern and there was Marv diving overboard, and Rad, and Jackie B, and Mo Snow. Had all these people been on his boat? He looked at the bow. Flames were leaping across his boat from one Coastliner to the other. Neither boat's pilot was trying to put out the fires. They each were on their knees praying.

The three boats were locked together, exploding in a series of blasts, as Joe bobbed in the water far astern. Startled, he opened his eyes to see the headlights of John Johns' pickup truck shining into the bed of Marv's camper top. John was honking his horn to wake up Joe and Marv for another morning of musky fishing.

Chapter 11

July 17th

Rad waited in the Malibu while Joe called in at the payphone at Straits and Myrtle avenues. She tried not to think about cigarettes. She smoked too much around Joe and was hoping to cut back. Quitting seemed impossible, but taking it a little easier was a goal she could accomplish. She tried to ignore discomfort, nerves, an overall prickly feeling concentrated in her neck and shoulders. A thought leaped into her mind, "Where the hell was Joe?"

The door opened, Joe sat down." A lot can change in a week. Let's go to Jackie B's. No, make that Serviceman's Park. Just drive up along the Straits."

"What did Andre say?"

"You know how he was uninterested in details, didn't care how I found stuff out? Well, now he wants to know why I spend so much money at a bait shop. He says catching people illegally crossing the border is not enough. He wants real results or he won't be able to fit me into his budget. I don't get it."

"Look, I don't need to turn in my mileage all the time if that'll help."

"No, you turn in your miles. This is the Federal Government. They've got all our tax money." Joe stared out the window. He was silent.

Joe and Rad had reached a point in their working relationship where they did not need to fill the void with conversation. They were comfortable enough with each other that they could be okay with silence.

Joe had begun to develop an itch in his mind. A thought, below the surface, had been gathering momentum, rolling around, seeking other ideas and data, to attach to itself. Andre had hammered him about money and spending it on beers at Jackie B's. Joe knew that Andre knew that the beers lubricated the slides down which the intel flowed. He was probably just out of a tough budget meeting or something. It was that other tidbit that was nettling Joe.

Multiple, at least two, sources in the Yemeni community around Pantherville had indicated something big was going to blow on a major American holiday. And it would blow in Pantherville. Joe needed to push harder to find out what was the target and what was the date. Labor Day and Thanksgiving were the only likely holidays when there would be open water. At the end of the boating season, Joe would be back in the construction business and on hiatus with Agent Andre. Of the two holidays, Labor Day seemed to be the obvious one. Joe brooded on what he knew and what he needed to find out. Andre wanted him to take more risks, to push Dumke harder. Of course, it wasn't Andre's five daughters that would be fatherless. Joe idly wondered if Andre had kids. The FBI agent had revealed nothing of himself.

Rad thought about the mission she was on, to watch Joe. And help him. And she thought about the mission Joe was on. What exactly was that? She didn't really know. She lit up a cigarette. One uncomfortable itchy feeling at a time was enough. When she cracked the window to let out smoke, Joe said, "Let's pull in here and watch the water go by. I need to think."

Joe walked over to a streamside bench. As he watched the water flow, he thought about what he knew; Dumke was brokering the purchase of boats. He had more money than he could have earned working. The Yemenis warned of something big—something going to blow. The people Dumke worked for were into alien smuggling and other stuff including murder and, he well knew, attempted murder. They operated out of Ontario but also in Pantherville. They seemed to use Dumke, but how much did they trust Mel?

He looked over at Rad, remembered something and said, "Hey, can you drop me at the Sherman boat launch? I gotta meet Marv."

Joe was uncomfortable when he slept in the back of Marv's truck. It was sticky and he was sweating.

The two Coastliners were squeezing him again but this time they were south of the Friendship Bridge. They were locked together being pushed by the current. The abutment at the eastern side of the center arch loomed ahead. Birds were circling overhead. Instead of gulls and terns, there were ravens and a hawk.

Joe took heart, the sight of a hawk was always good for him, but ravens indicated trickery, trouble as often as not. The raft of boats plowed toward the bridge. A fire broke out on the thirty-two foot cabin cruiser. The flames leaped from the Coastliner to his Whaler as if spread by gasoline. Joe raised his eyes to the bridge. The hawk dove. There, on the ledge, where the concrete abutment gave way to the steel bridge girders, was Mo Snow and next to him a large black bear. Mo leaped into the air, turned into a heron, flapped his wings and flew west into Canada. The bear growled but Joe heard a deep voice say, "Brother, you must stop this." The hawk lifted Joe by the shoulders and carried him so high into the sky that the boats and the bridge and the two countries were gone.

Chapter 12

July 20th

Rad often felt that she was no more than Joe's driver in this job. That feeling was strong now as she wheeled the "roach coach" portable snack and coffee service truck into an access drive in front of one of the mansions on Mingo Avenue in Pantherville. These mansions had almost all given over to private clubs, insurance offices, and stock brokerages. They had impressive yards and gardens that were cared for by professional landscaping crews. It was one of the crew chiefs from *Spring Peeper's Lawn & Garden Keepers* that Joe wanted to speak to. Bobbi Eberle, an attractive young woman, approached Joe's side of the truck shouldering a weed whacker and pushing her safety glasses up into her tightly braided hair. Before going to open the side of the truck to serve the workers, crowding around for their sweet rolls, doughnuts, and coffee, Rad did her usual swift calculation of Bobbi's body type.

Eberle was blond and fair-skinned, though ruddy from working outside in the summer. She had a swimmer's body, broad shouldered, flat chested and strong in the hips and legs. Her legs were shapely though somewhat mannish in aspect. She was obviously a strong woman, used to physical work, who had no difficulty leading her all-male crews. She was running three separate crews on Mingo Avenue this fine summer day. Rad noticed her genuine warm smile as she greeted the peripatetic Joe Gaspe, who seemed to know somebody from almost every profession. Joe and Ms. Eberle walked off where they could talk privately.

Rad waited on the crews. She endured their witless suggestive repartee as they showed off in front of each other and the new coffee girl. There were only two women in the sixteen-member crew. The Americans were young kids and stoners, while most of the older men appeared to be Hispanic.

Later Joe related to Rad what Bobbi had told him.

"She says that her landscape company and four others were purchased this spring. That Mel Dumke owns two companies and a total of seven crews even though he knows next to nothing about the business. She also said, she didn't like Mel too much." Joe chuckled. "What does odious mean anyway? Nothing good I'll bet."

"Worse than contemptible, I think. How'd you meet her?" Rad asked.

"Enough about that. There is a moneyman who installed Dumke and he's the one who came up with the lame name and logo. She thought maybe the frog is lucky to Chinese people."

"The money man is Chinese? That could explain a few things about Derek Chang's murder. The landscaping business might also be a way to occupy some of the illegals before they are moved inland. Though, as you've said, with two Chinese restaurants in every town they'd have no trouble hiding people."

"Ya think? But all the illegals are not Chinese, far from it."

"All right, Joe, these illegal immigrants could be shuttled in and out of landscape company vans with no one the wiser. That strategy would work from spring through Christmas time."

"Yep. And keeping Dumke on the loose may lead us to the next level of operator."

"The next level—you mean that you think there is more than one level above Dumke?"

"You know Rad, we have stopped some shipments of contraband—that's what your uncle told me they called escaped slaves during the civil war—but some must be getting through, too. And we have found no terrorists, as such, at all. This operation, which we know is too sophisticated for Dumke, probably goes beyond the Chinese American who is Mel's boss. It stands to reason that that guy is being squeezed hard one level up."

"Chinese people revere their ancestors and men have an obligation to their mothers that borders on obsession. I'll bet Dumke's boss is just being blackmailed and there's a more sinister power pushing him around." Rad was getting the same idea as Joe.

"Ya think?"

Joe didn't like getting bogged down in details and he considered any contact with Agent Andre a detail. He was wary since his earlier dressing down on the phone. He and Rad went to the downtown mall to meet the FBI man. Joe left Rad in the coffee shop while he and Thomas Andre strolled and Joe made his report. Andre had forgotten his demands from the previous phone call. He made no mention of them.

The mall was a sad one; many of the stores had closed. The customers of stores catering to the office crowd refused to force their way through the roving crowds of teenagers and twenty-somethings that circled the mall. Fewer and fewer businesses were viable each year. No one bothered Joe and Thomas as they chatted and walked, although some noted the incongruity of the working class white man and the dapper black businessman, deep in conversation.

"Somebody put up the money for Mel Dumke to be buying landscaping companies. Last November he was living in a ten year old Buick, unemployed and homeless, and griping about everyone and everything."

"The purchase of a viable business is a matter of public record. We can find out who bought it but it will probably turn out to be Dumke," Agent Andre replied.

"He had to write a check. Someone had to pay him money to deposit in his account to buy those businesses."

"It may be a dummy corporation, but we will know in a day or two."

"Okay, I think the landscaping thing is only part of the deal but it does get them moving around without being suspicious and they get trailers to load with whatever. And who pays attention to a Puerto Rican mowing the grass."

"Puerto Rico is a territory of the United States. But I take your point regarding Hispanic men and landscaping work."

"I'll keep digging." Joe was ready to break this off. He liked Agent Andre but had never been comfortable around authority figures.

"Remember, time marches on. The Yemenis, at least the reliable ones, insist that something is imminent."

"Do you pay these guys by the tip?" Joe thought that was humorous; Andre didn't agree.

"I enjoyed our little chat, Joe. Don't be a stranger." They went their separate ways.

Joe had dreamed of the bird flight with he and Mo Snow, hawk and heron, to the jungles of Central America several times. *His dream now started with the travel accomplished and hawk, heron, and raven perched on a branch observing the dismal swamp and raven clucking and tsk-tsking and tut-tutting as the two cousins watched the swarm of frogs below. The poison frogs guarded the huge red eft, as big as a rolling pin, from being seen or even approached by any predator.*

In the dream, Joe and Mo watched and the raven croaked. As the dream would dissolve with no action, Joe could see the ugly misshapen head of Mel Dumke leer mockingly at him.

Moses Snow

Chapter 13

July 24th

Interns Ger Blog, Kyle Buchalter, and Rad Loonch were seated on one side of the conference table. Their three bosses were on the other side. Each intern had filed a report prior to their midsummer conference and the reports had been read and evaluated. This was the review session and two of the three bosses were grinning with satisfaction. In a dark corner of the room sat Thomas Andre, with a thin notebook and an elegant pen, taking occasional notes.

Rad knew her report would embarrass her boss. She could tell by the dagger eyes she was receiving during the review of the other reports, that Hubert Hilliard was angry. Her report, sitting in a binder in front of him, was thin. The binders in front of the other bosses were huge, chock-a-block with photographs and tables, and interlarded with sidebars culled from research in libraries and on the Internet. Rad stole the odd glance at Agent Andre. He smiled with his eyes, as if to say, "Don't worry, be happy."

Ger and Kyle were inseparable. They had shared research and split their information to support each other's reports. Most importantly, they had laid on the compliments to their respective agencies like a spread of peanut butter on one of Elvis Presley's famous sandwiches. Nothing pleases a bureaucrat more than the feeling that the world would stop without his particular specialty. What Ger and Kyle had learned in college was to feed the teacher what he wants, and complement as well as compliment his narrow thinking.

Shlomo Antontrowicz beamed with pride as he read in a lisping monotone the synopsis of Ger's report. Ger adjusted his shoulders, to seem even larger, as he was praised. This was no mean feat for a man six-foot-six and four hundred pounds. "In conclusion, I feel that Gerhard Blog has done a masterful job of summarizing the comprehensive sustained approach to Homeland Security of the Pantherville station of the United States Army Corps of Engineers. I am going to make sure my superiors and their superiors, all the way to Washington, are made aware of this exemplary work. In addition, the parts of this fine summary that are not too sensitive will be covered in an article in the Pantherville Press in an upcoming issue. Great job, Ger." At this point, Shlomo applauded his intern and was joined in polite applause by the others present.

Delmar Norris, not quite the academic that Shlomo was, with a background in military service and law enforcement, was less pedantic in his evaluation of Kyle's report. Leafing through the binders, Rad noticed that, while Ger's was heavy on charts and graphs and tables, Kyle's was strong on pictures with numerous shots of Coast Guard boats speeding along, up on plane. Rather than read Kyle's summary, Delmar said, "This is the best report from the best intern we've ever had and shows convincingly why the expansion of the Pantherville Station of the United States Coast Guard was important and should continue. I concur with Sol that these reports should be sent up the line. I have arranged for excerpts and a few photographs," here he held up one of himself in front of one of the Guard's Rigid Hull Inflatables, "will be in the Sunday Supplement of the Pantherville Press." The polite applause for Kyle was more subdued than that for Ger had been, since it was not led so heartily by Norris.

Hubert Hilliard cleared his throat several times as he opened Rad's exceedingly slim volume. He seemed hesitant to start. Rad glanced at Thomas Andre who clicked his pen and concentrated on his notebook. The summary page was a simple list. After a one-sentence introduction the list had seven entries. Hubert slowly read each entry and paused inviting Rad to comment. She declined each invitation.

"Number one, helped form a network of information providers," pause. "Number two, created a reporting protocol for those in the network," pause. "Number three, helped an agent in place report to the Coast Guard key intelligence that prevented the landing of two groups of illegal aliens," pause. "Number four, moved well along investigating leads on other things," pause. "Does this mean terrorism?" Hubert looked over his spectacles at her. His visage was grim.

"I'd rather not say." Rad stared down her boss. When he looked down at the report, she glanced at Thomas Andre. His nod was barely perceptible.

"Number five, have been unable to stop several instances of illegal immigration," pause. The Army Corps boss, seated beside Hilliard, let out an audible sigh. Hilliard moved on. "Number six, have developed leads on the financial backers behind the people smuggling of illegal Chinese immigrants and others," pause.

"Would you care to inform us about the details of this?"

"Not at this time." Rad was nothing if not taciturn.

"Number seven, have identified the existence of at least one 'mole' in the local Homeland Security apparatus," pause. "Ms. Loonch, this cannot stand there without explanation." Thomas Andre cleared his throat loudly just as Rad rose to the bait.

She spoke while looking at the FBI man and ignoring her boss. "There are several threads moving forward due to the agent in place with whom I am working. Each agency should look to see that its own house is in order." She dropped her eyes to the table and raised them with a look of defiance that bored into the forehead of Shlomo Antontrowicz.

Hubert Hilliard neither led any cheers for Rad, nor praised her work. He merely adjourned the meeting and hurried from the room. As she was leaving Rad was stopped by Andre's light touch on her arm. He said one word to her, "Perfect."

The interns decided to go out for a drink after their reviews. To prove that there were no hard feelings, Ger and Kyle went with Rad's choice and they ended up at the barroom of Jackie B's. The two men had thought, by the name, that this was some cool club of which they'd never heard. They wrinkled their noses at the smell of dead minnows, always just under the surface, in the barroom. Neither intern minded the two-dollars-for-all-you-can-drink Labatt's Blue deal, and they soon were able to ignore the smell.

"I can't believe you turned in such a lame report. You guys have been doing stuff, why not claim your props." Kyle looked to Rad for an answer.

Rad's face was not expressive as she quoted Joe Gaspe and said, "Details confuse bosses, it's better to give them as few as possible."

"But your boss was pissed off. We made our life easy by pleasing our fearless leaders."

"Yeah, and you guys are back in college in a few weeks. I graduated and I'm in this job for the near future. Eyewash isn't what matters. I need to produce results. The guy I really need to please was the guy in the corner."

"That black guy? Is he FBI? What's his real job anyway?"

Rad didn't answer that question.

Moses X Snow joined Rad at the round table at that moment. He gave her shoulder a friendly squeeze. He sat and looked over the two interns, during Rad's introductions, with that impassive face considered the stereotype of an Indian. After staring at Ger, then Kyle, Mo said, "How." They looked at him wide eyed, for a few seconds, before he broke into a disarming grin. Mo turned to Rad and asked, "Are Joe and Marvin catching any muskies? Does Joe ever take you out for the big fish?"

Rad patted his burly arm, asked after his health and said, "The only time he took me out, it was so rough I thought I'd puke myself inside out."

Mo Snow smiled widely and said, "That cousin of mine never did know when to fish, or how neither." Mo laughed heartily at his jest. He reached into his kit bag and retrieved a Thermos and poured himself a drink. Steam rose from the liquid.

"What are you drinking, a hot toddy?" Kyle was trying to act nonchalant but his amazement, at the Mohawk's appearance and demeanor, showed in his nervous question.

"Clear tea. I'm a Mohawk from Canada, eh? Did I hear you asking about my friend Agent Thomas?"

"Is that what he is, an FBI agent?" Kyle was inquisitive. Ger was thirsty and took the three Schooners up to the tap for refills.

"These terrorists who are at war with my three countries are very upsetting to my cousin, Joe Gaspe, Radleigh's friend. He works with Agent Thomas to defeat them. Radleigh is the assistant to Joe. Agent Thomas helps to keep others out of the warrior's path that Joe is on." Mo always used first names and usually did not shorten them except with family members.

"Three countries? Warrior's Path? Assistant?" Kyle looked at Rad with respect in his eyes. "I guess those reports of ours are pretty small potatoes. "

"Mo is a member of the Flint People, the Mohawks, a nation of the Haudenosaunee, the people of the longhouse, you'd call them Iroquois. The Six Nation Confederacy is his first nation. He lives on the Canadian side of the reservation at Akwesasne. The larger part of that Rez is in New York State. Hence, he is a person of three nations. By the way do you know why they are called Mohawks?" Rad was enjoying showing off her anthropology background while cluing the boys in.

"No, why?"

"That was the name that their adversaries called them, because they were such feared warriors. It means cannibal." Rad played this for the shock value.

"My three nations will one day soon be one nation again." Mo said, resuming the impassive expression that was normal for him. As he held his tea before his lips, he appeared to be meditating.

Kyle was dumbstruck. He stared at Mo and then Rad. Ger drained his schooner and looked at the others' drinks. They were not ready so he moved to the tap for one refill this time.

"Agent Thomas is a man of power in many ways and he keeps his friends close and his adversaries even closer." Mo was deliberately being obtuse, since he wanted the interns to know, but knew they were not capable of really knowing. "He is of the real world. An eagle."

Jackie B poked his head around the corner and said to Mo, "Your shipment checks out, come back in the store and I will pay your invoice, in US dollars." The last words were emphasized in an ironic way.

Mo turned to Rad, said, "You keep Moneto with you, Radleigh." He nodded to the two fellows and picked up his otter skin satchel and was gone through the bait shop door.

"Wow, I wish I got to work with a really cool guy like that." Kyle never hid how easily impressed he was. Gerhard Blog belched. Rad couldn't hold her face closed: she beamed.

After her day of evaluation with the interns, Rad was back at the Park and Ride in Muskedaigua to pick up Joe. She was waiting, looking for Marv's truck to drop him off, when she heard a rapping on the window. There was Joe on foot, no Marv, and no truck. She hit her unlock button and Joe slipped in.

"How'd you get here?"

"My wife dropped me off a block back, that Marv is a full-time partner but a part time pain in the neck. You don't want to know what kind of trouble he's in. It involves the police and everything." Joe seemed nervous to Rad.

Rad put the Malibu into gear, looked in the rear view mirror, and a minivan pulled across her path just before she pressed the accelerator. She couldn't go forward or back, so she returned the shifter to park.

Joe said, "Uh-oh," at the same time that Rad said, "What in the world is this?"

"That's my wife. I'll handle this." Joe got out of the Malibu. A woman had bailed out of the minivan in her housecoat. She was obviously angry and headed for Rad's side of the car. Even without makeup, and in a shapeless gown, Rad could see that she would be an attractive woman if she'd calm down. Five children had added some pounds, but she had handled the transition well.

"Katie, Katie, let me explain." Joe was going around between the two cars when his youngest daughter said, "Hi Daddy." She had crawled across the seats and was leaning out the driver's window. Momentarily distracted, Joe said "Hey sweetie." He gave her one of his disarming winks.

Kate Gaspe was looking down at Rad and she was boiling mad. Her hands were on her hips, her face was compressed into a scowl, and her lower lip was thrust forward in a pout. She stared at Rad with the eyes of a murderess. "Who are you, his latest floozie?"

"Ma'am, I'm on the job here."

Kate was not an accomplished hater and she wavered immediately. As Rad began to speak, Kate's arms went from her hips across her chest. She defended her heart from the arrows of explanation headed her way. She suddenly feared that her defense would be unsuccessful.

Joe took another step, "Kate, don't yell at her. I can explain what's going on."

"Daddy, Mommy, no fighting." Little Lucy scrunched up her face ready to cry. She was only four, but she'd learned how to manipulate her parents and diffuse their battles. Joe hesitated and looked from her to Kate and back to Lucy.

"I'm gonna give this home wrecker a piece of my mind, Joe, and you"re not going to stop me!"

Lucy began letting out a well-practiced plaintive wail. Joe wavered and turned to her and opened his arms. Lucy reached for him and said, "No fighting." This was Daddy's familiar instruction, when any of his five daughters were going at it with each other.

Rad got out of the car and stood up. Kate's height advantage, when she was next to a seated Rad, disappeared when the taller Rad looked down upon her. It was a scene that required order and Rad took her opportunity.

"Joe, shut up," she cut off his protest to his wife. "You take your daughter over there," she pointed at a little bus shelter with a park bench. Lucy sniffled a couple of times, smiled at her father and he at her, and they did as they were told.

"Mrs. Gaspe, there's some things you need to be told that will clear up a misunderstanding. We'll chat over here." Rad led Kate to the rear of the Malibu. Separated from Joe, Kate's anger began to defuse.

It took fifteen minutes for Radleigh Loonch, reluctant but capable instructor, to explain to Kate Gaspe that her husband was working for Homeland Security, that Rad was his driver-assistant, that she was not his sex toy and could repel any advances he tried. Kate knew her man. Rad ascribed the motive of protecting his family to Joe's reticence to tell his wife any of what he'd been doing for the last few months. Rad's firm, friendly, and cogent explanation calmed Kate. The two women shared a cigarette, even though Kate was not a smoker, and the crisis was over.

"Why didn't you tell her what you could, instead of leaving her totally in the dark?" Rad was behind the wheel and they were on the way to Pantherville. "I had wanted to tell you about my performance review and your cousin Mo's meeting with my intern counterparts. I didn't feel like mediating a marital spat."

"I couldn't think of a way to tell her so she wouldn't worry, I'm not a good liar. How was Mo Snow?"

"I suppose you don't think you get enough practice lying."

Joe admitted that she had him there.

Chapter 14

July 30th

*T*he coins were now medals with silk ribbons attached for wearing around one's neck. Joe was still straightening them on the way to a fishing trip but now Mo was speaking to him.

"These were given by the old man who wore his own hair. The bear man. One silver disc went to Cook and one silver disc went to Brant. The bear man knew the power of the Mohawks. He was pledging them to an alliance with the Sunrise People. I know where one disc is. Do you know whether your mother kept the other?"

It was Rudi Loonch who had told him about Ben Franklin—the man who wore his own hair—having a prominent role in the Albany Conference of 1754. He had also alluded to the medals with King George on them that had been given to prominent Mohawks as a symbol of the burnishing of the covenant chain of friendship between the English (Sunrise People) and the Mohawks (Real People).

Bits of experience intruded on dreams and modified dreams and amended dreams. There was no irony in Joe's mind that a self-taught non-Indian, Rudi, provided details that affected his dreams. To his way of thinking, Rudi Loonch occupied a place in his pathway for the specific purpose of enhancing some dream or event or both.

King George's medals handled by Ben Franklin, not Franklin coins, that is what recurred in his dreams every few days. This was close to an Aha moment for Joe, but not quite.

When Joe stopped at the barroom portion of Big Haul there was only one person there. It was Rudyard Loonch. He had a take-out fried chicken box on the table in front of him, a book open at his elbow, and a schooner of beer before him. He looked up and smiled in his way. His mouth only turned up slightly at the corners but his eyes lit up in recognition at the arrival of his partner.

"Whatcha reading?" Joe saw several books on the table. In exchange for swamping out the place, sweeping, mopping, washing the schooners, Jackie B let Rudyard use the room as his research library, taking the corner table and reading, writing, and researching for hours at a time.

"Just looking something up." Rudyard turned the book over and Joe saw that it was a Mohawk language dictionary. He never knew what to expect from Rudi and was seldom disappointed.

"My mother was a Mohawk, you know. My stepmother, too." Joe saw that Rudyard was impressed.

"Then you might know why I find them so fascinating." Rudyard waited to be told to go on. He was often wary about talking too much. He didn't wish to be a preacher. Joe's head nodded yes, but his eyes said no.

"I know many Mohawks today, and other people of the long-house, but I never learned a lot about the past of the tribe. Since 1990 I've kept up with them. My cousin Mo and Uncle Mike have taught me some words and ideas." Joe said.

"I read a philosopher once who said that the people who occupy a land, the conquerors, eventually become just like the people they conquer." Loonch left the concept out there, that the environment makes the residents trend in a certain way. "I don't know, but it could be argued that the Iroquois League had a profound impact on the US and continues to do so today. Even though they were a small group in population, they affected the development of our whole country."

"Uncle Mike thinks they are more important than they appear to be. But, he's a Seneca."

"The Mohawks were the leaders of the Six Nations because they were the warriors who led the way in conquering all the eastern tribes. The Mohawks, your people, were so fierce that whole tribes of other Indians would surrender to a handful of Mohawk warriors. But two hundred and fifty years of constant warfare, even though they usually won the battles, nearly wiped out the tribe. They did not have enough members to expand their numbers through natural increase, so they kidnapped and adopted other people, white, red, and black, even a few Chinese to try to improve their numbers. They were the original melting pot. It didn't matter your race or culture, when you were adopted you became a Mohawk. Interesting, huh?"

"We need to talk more about this sometime, but right now I was wondering what you'd heard lately from my old buddy Mel Dumke. Does he still come in here and blow off?" Joe had heard some things that were rolling around in his mind unattached and he wanted to see if he could get them to stick together.

"You know Joe, when I'm sweeping up around, or washing glasses behind the bar, people talk like I'm not even there. They'll be reticent when I'm sitting here with my books, but cackle like biddies when I'm working. Of course, with my books my mind is occupied and with a broom I hear everything, but they act as if it's just the opposite."

"Dumke? You heard anything?"

"He's been buying boats brokered by Ian Drakulitch. He's been bragging about all the money he has. He drives a couple of different vans and trucks. One is a landscape company van; but he doesn't seem to work much."

"He say why he wants more than one boat?"

"I don't think the boats are for him. He said something about rich Canadians. You know, this time of year the landscapers work dawn 'til dark, but Dumke just seems to be dropping in during the day all the time. No schedule, if you know what I mean."

"I heard he bought a landscaping company, did you hear that?"

"He went from living out of a ten year old Buick to owning a company. Do you suppose a rich uncle died?"

"I think he has a benefactor but I don't think it's his uncle. Don't tell him I asked about him, OK?" Joe looked at Rudyard, judged the return look he got, and laughed, "Heh, heh, heh, you wouldn't talk to him would you?"

"Some people, Joe, are beneath contempt."

Joe left with a couple more ball bearings rolling around in the milk jug of his mind.

Chapter 15

August 7th

Marv Ankara was in a neighborhood place, the kind where they do shots and beers and don't replace the glasses with clean ones unless asked. The bar was full, not crammed, busy with serious drinkers. There were only a few women present and they were escorted.

Marv had had a few rounds when an old acquaintance from the Straits Musky Club sidled up to him and ordered drinks. It was Mel Dumke. Marv knew him as a former charter captain who had wrecked his uninsured boat on Scull reef and sold off his musky fishing gear. Buying that gear had enabled Marv and Joe to get into musky fishing on the cheap. That was how Joe liked to do everything except build his custom wooden rods.

"Hi Marv, long time no see. How've you been, brother?"

"Mel, where you been keeping yourself?"

"Here and there, trying to make ends meet."

"Same thing with me. Thanks for the Blue."

"I thought I remembered that was your brand. Say, where's Joe Gaspe these days?"

"He's here. He went over to that kid's club around the corner or outside to smoke. I'd rather drink than smoke but Joe's got fancy friends these days and he's smoking with a bunch out there."

"Fancy friends, huh?" Dumke could see an opening for information. "Whattya mean?"

"He used to be my partner—sure we had our beefs but we were buds. Now he hardly has time to fish with me in that hot new boat of his. A Boston Whaler. Do you believe that? And he's got this posse of hangers on—a college girl and two young guys, one is a huge guy—another college kid, too big for the boat. They are always lurking around. And secret stuff, meetings and errands he calls them. I'll be honest with you. He ticks me off these days." Marv took a long pull at his beer and emptied it. Mel Dumke had bought him two more Blues. They were lined up, cold and dripping condensation.

When Marv had reached for the new one, but before he'd taken a pull, Dumke said, "Secret stuff, that's tough when a buddy betrays you."

"Oh, he hasn't betrayed me. He just don't have no time for fishin' and shooting guns and bar-hopping and stuff."

"He say who he's having all these meetings with?"

"That's something else that bugs me, he keeps me out of the loop. It's important, though. It's the government that gave him the boat. I think he's working with the cops—anti-terrorism would be my guess. We always gotta make calls from certain payphones like the one at Straits and Myrtle. I don't know, he's still my best fishin' partner, but I feel like he doesn't trust me."

"Ain't that kinda girly? Worrying about your feelings." This came from Jackie Bertwilliger who had just pulled up the barstool on the other side of Marv. Marv looked at him with fierce eyes before he recognized him and smiled.

"You breaking balls again, Jackie B?"

Dumke took the opportunity to make his exit, excusing himself to go to the men's room. Bertwilliger looked past Marv towards the door. He saw Dumke speak to a man at the end of the bar, ignore the passage to the men's room, and leave the bar.

"Marv, you gotta watch what you say about Joe. Dumke is a snake and he bites."

"I didn't say nothin.' Nothin' much anyway."

"It don't matter now." Jackie pulled out his cell phone and said, "I'll be right back," as he stepped away to a quieter area.

The interns, Rad, Ger, and Kyle, were with Joe and Mo Snow on the outdoor patio of the Huron Street House of Blues. They were on the edge of the young crowd that was sampling the vibrant nightlife of Pantherville. The college-age and hip crowd from the eight surrounding counties crammed themselves into one three-block strip of clubs and bars. All the clubs were overcrowded, sweaty, deafening, early twenty-first century examples of wretched excess. There were more tattoos, pierced flesh, exposed navels, and butt cleavage in this quarter mile than Mo Snow ever believed could exist while living on his rural Quebec farm.

"My partner Melvin Loonch says, 'There's enough people trying to do you harm, why would you pay someone to stick needles in you or poke holes in you?'" Joe was winking at Rad as he quoted her father. She was rolling her eyes. "He says his number one goal is to avoid pain in his life, heh, heh, heh. A good man, he makes me laugh."

Joe noticed that Mo couldn't get used to all the tight shirts, gaudy jewelry, and makeup on the constant parade of slim women. To his mind, they looked like starving whores who seemed to want men to treat them as such, with their skimpy clothes, their language, and their dirty dancing. From shared dreaming, Joe knew how Mo thought. Sexual energy in Mohawk dreaming was both explicit and subtly lurking below the surface. Though Mo preferred women to be better fed than these, his libido responded to the waves of sexuality washing along the channel that was Huron Street.

In the corner of the smoking patio, the five were far enough from the loud blues music to hear each other's conversation.

"I've gotta go back around the corner and pick up Marv. Can you fill these guys in on what's happening Mo?'

"I will do so." Mo sounded confident, though with his head on a swivel looking at nubile young women, Joe wasn't so sure.

It took a few minutes for Joe to sidle past the press of bodies and get to the side door onto Benjamin Street. He was glad to get into the cool outside air and stopped at the corner of the building to light a cigarette. He planned to take an extra few minutes going around the corner in order to finish his smoke. Leaning his back against the building with his right knee bent and the sole of his shoe flat against the wall, he struck a pose as he watched the revelers, fewer here on Benjamin but still a crowd, passing. Joe was a married man who, though flirtatious, was usually faithful to Kate, but he hadn't been struck blind. Two stunning Asian girls, completely tarted-up to look like sex machines, came up to him from the alley side. They moved in close, enveloping Joe with their scent, one brought her small breasts, barely concealed by a halter top, right against his left arm while the other moved her face close to his and said, "Hey, Joe, are you a man who likes it outdoors?"'

Joe had begun to speak, when they jumped quickly backwards, their expressions changed from smoky sexy to matter-of-fact businesslike. Before he could react, he was grabbed by powerful hands and bull-rushed down the alley to his right. He tried to turn and was rapped hard, with a club, on the left side, on and over his ear. Joe was in trouble. Through the ringing in his ear he heard one man say, "Say nothing and you'll come out of this alive."

"No way!" Joe's mind worked fast. In crisis, time seemed to slow down for him. Things happened too fast to counter physically, but his Mohawk mind moved thoughts through it in sequence, making then comprehensible. His head rang with the beat of a tinny drum. The two thugs alternately marched and dragged him down the alley toward three men wrapped from head to toe, like Arabs, with only their eyes showing. The two on the ends of the line held aluminum baseball bats. The man in the center spoke to them in a guttural language Joe did not understand. When Joe was shoved in front of them, each bat hit a leg with a hard blow buckling one knee then the other. Hurt, Joe quickly fell onto all fours. He wanted to scream. He held it in.

"You should have remained a carpenter, Joe Gaspe," This from the center "Arab" whose voice had a distinctly English accent. The next two blows, one from each side, hit him on the biceps near the shoulder. Joe was driven face down to the pavement by these hard hits. He rolled on his face, managed a look back, saw the guys who had grabbed him guarding the entrance to the alley, preventing escape.

"Go back to your trade or we will kill you." The Englishman spoke and the "Arabs" swung. Joe blocked two shots to his head with his forearms. He knew his head couldn't take many blows with those bats. He raised his head to look at his attackers, and saw an aura above his tormentor. That man's next sentence slowed down so much in his mind that Joe heard merely a reverberating growl.

The aura was dark violet with red at the edges and a huge raven sat, black, at its center with an orange–yellow beak that looked like two tomahawks clacking together as each word was spoken by the English Arab. Before the slow growling sentence was done, and the next blows were struck, the raven squawked and the aura became a blur.

Rad and the other interns were listening to Mo Snow. He explained how he and Joe, cousins on the Mohawk side of Joe's lineage, had met as warriors at the Kanesatake Reservation anti-development protest at Oka in 1990. The Mohawk warriors had defied both Quebec and Canada and blocked the bridge at St. Mercier to try involving the USA. The aftermath of the protest was one of the reasons that Joe had a problem with Canadian officials.

"He was an active radical then but has settled down some."

"How is it you and he have remained close?" Rad was ever the anthropologist.

"We are both of the wolf clan and we both have totem birds as our communicating spirit. Mine is the heron, Joe's the hawk. That is why we can meet in dreams—Mohawk e-mail, Joe calls it," Mo said this last with a twinkling eye and a broad smile as he looked directly at Rad. The other two interns were so skeptical of all this, and had imbibed so much, that they did not notice the change suddenly come over Mo's face as if a shade had been drawn. He fell from laughter to trance for a mere few seconds. With a shake of all his features, he said loudly, "Joe's in trouble. Now! Come!"

Mo charged like a pulling guard. He slammed his broad shoulder into the wooden fence that surrounded the patio. He crashed right through the fence and rolled into the sidewalk, completed his roll to a running position, and turned right around the corner into the alley beside The House of Blues. Rad looked around to judge the reaction to Mo's destruction, ducked through the hole in the fence, and followed at a run to see what was up. Kyle said to Ger, enjoying his buzz, "Cool!" and the two interns followed at a walk. Several patrons and people on the street, hearing the crash as Mo took out the fence, followed. Everyone was attracted to commotion and excitement.

Joe's slowing of time was a familiar dream state for him and he could sort out both the blurred visuals and the reverberating sounds.

"We will end your infidel life before you ruin our plans." This was what the leader said just before the third round of ball bat blows rained down on Joe. The English Arab noticed Joe looking up past him, toward the gargoyle on the nearby building's cornice. He turned to look. This caused his last words to fade out since they were directed away from Joe.

Looking past his attacker, Joe saw that the raven being driven out of the circle of aura by a hawk of heroic size, slashing at the trickster with talon and beak.

This was going to be the end of his life if Joe didn't do something. He tried to drive forward to tackle the nearest man, the speaker. Numbness caused his knees to collapse under him and he could barely crawl. He was only able to squirm and wiggle to try getting inside the blows from his assailants.

The last blow, from the man on the right, glanced off Joe's bruised ear and bounced off his shoulder. Though this swing knocked his arm down and his shoulder hit the pavement, it was a milder blow than the others. Joe heard the other bat clatter to the ground without striking him. As his mind slipped into an unconscious state, he heard a familiar cry.

Rad came around the corner of the House of Blues to see a sprinting Mo Snow split the double team block of two burly men. He rammed a forearm into each chin snapping their heads back as he screamed, "AAIIYEEEEE!!! He barreled over and past the startled thugs and headed straight for the three men assaulting a man on the ground. That man being beaten, she realized with horror, was Joe Gaspe. The charge of a screaming crazy Indian panicked the assailants and they took off down the alley away from Mo.

Rad ran past the two guards who were scrambling to their feet and watched Mo leap over Joe's body, and pursue the retreating Arabs. Mo tackled the slowest, smacked the man's head on the pavement with his forearm, grabbed him by the hair to lift his head, and smacked him again with his forearm. After hitting this man three times he dropped him and ran down the alley after the others. Mo screamed in triumph.

Rad knelt beside Joe, who seemed barely conscious when she turned him over. He opened his right eye just as Rad heard the krr,krr,krr sound of a hawk. Joe gave an exaggerated wink, said, "Saved by the hawk," and passed out.

Back at the entrance to the alley, the two guards were gone but Ger and Kyle were watching. Kyle said, "This is so cool!"

Rad yelled at them, "Dial 911. Joe needs an ambulance."

"That's Joe?"

"Dial 911, you dork!" Rad let Joe lie there, breathing shallowly. She looked up to see Mo's victim struggle to his feet, bloody, but ready to run. With a sense of purpose that surprised her, Rad stepped right up to him and emptied her one-ounce container of Mace directly into his bloody face. He screamed, clawed at his eyes, and stumbled around the alley, bouncing off walls, doorways, and garbage cans. Rad noticed that the assailant did not have the beard of a fundamentalist Muslim, and though dressed like an Arab on the outside, he had on jeans and a t-shirt underneath.

Mo returned up the alley and said, "They got away. The hawk will track them." He casually picked up one of the bats and took a home run swing at the head of the Maced assailant. With a sickening thwack his head opened up a new gusher and he fell against a doorway. His body slumped into a sitting position against a padlocked steel door. He looked like a drunk sleeping one off.

Mo looked at Rad blankly, knelt beside Joe who was still unconscious and said, "I don't need to be here if the authorities show, Joe. We will find these evildoers. Your helpers and I will find them."

He turned to Rad, "Please take my cousin to Dr. Bramton," He handed her a business card, "Leave this place to the dead man."

"Is he dead?" Rad inclined her head toward the doorway.

"Oh, yes." Mo turned to go back down the alley into the dark. Rad grabbed his arm and handed him the container of Mace. He took it without a word and loped down the alley in that all-day-running gait for which Mohawks are renowned.

Turning to the other two interns, Rad heard the krrr, krrr, krrr of the hawk again. "Kyle, get the car. Ger, help me get Joe into the car; we've got to take him to the doctor."

"There's an ambulance coming, aren't we gonna wait for it?" Ger was still shaky from witnessing the battle.

"They can work on him," she said nodding her head toward the attacker in the doorway, "Even though he's a goner."

"Wow, a dead guy." Kyle said.

"Kyle, get the car." Rad gave orders naturally.

Within a few minutes they'd bundled a reviving Joe Gaspe into the car and headed for the Doctor's office.

Chapter 16

August 8th

Rad was sitting in the waiting room across the coffee table from Kyle and Ger, thinking how she'd have ditched these guys if they hadn't all driven to Muskedaigua in the same vehicle. It was four AM and the boys were suffering. Kyle was hung over and Ger was hungry. Periodically, Kyle would moan and lean his head on Ger's shoulder while half-asleep. Ger, with surprising gentleness, would tenderly move Kyle's head away and stare lovingly at the snack machine that was just outside the door.

Rad had been busy on the phone during the forty-minute drive to the Muskedaigua Family Clinic. First, she had to rouse Dr. Bramton—Joe's personal physician and repair specialist, his wife's best friend—and agree on a time to meet her at the clinic. Second, she had to find Joe's wife and explain to her why Rad had the woman's bruised and battered husband in her back seat. Then, she'd had to call Marv and tell him that Joe wouldn't be meeting him for the ride back to Coleman, the suburb of Muskedaigua where they both lived. Fourth, she had to call the pager number of Agent Andre and await his return call. She regretted that she had no way to contact Mo Snow. Her impression of Mo's qualities as a man and a person of power deepened each time she encountered him.

Rad, unable to contact Joe's wife, Kate, had left answering machine messages. It wasn't until after they'd been at the clinic a half hour that they she received the first of two return calls. This was from Joe's eldest daughter, Amelia, the estranged one. This had been a challenging conversation that involved a lot of questioning as to who Rad was and what she was doing with Amelia's Dad. Eventually, it worked out that she had to get someone to watch the younger children and get a ride but she would be down to the clinic soon. Her mother was out of town visiting a sick sister.

The second call had been Agent Andre answering his page. He had listened calmly to Rad's heated description of the attempt on Joe's life, thanked Rad for keeping in touch and hung up. As usual the FBI man made no statement of what he intended to do.

A few minutes later Rad had been in to see Joe, who sat on an examining table with his head wrapped in a bandage, a gown on, and Nurse Greury wrapping the second knee in a pressure dressing. His left eye, black and blue, was swollen nearly shut, both his arms were bruised, angry red turning to sickly blue, from elbow to shoulder, yet he smiled at Rad and said, "I guess I should have ducked."

The outer door rattled as it opened. A sleepy eyed teenaged girl swept in, followed by an older man, who looked so much like Joe that he had to be his brother. Kyle raised his head said, "Whazzup? Ouch! OW oooo," and immediately lolled his head back and began to snore. Ger looked for a lunchbox in the hand of either person. Rad stepped into the waiting room, and offered her hand, which was ignored, to Joe's daughter. Amelia asked, "Where is that horse's ass?" And seeing him, she burst through the glass door into the examining room. Rad noticed Joe's face take on a sheepish expression of shame as his daughter lit into him, loudly. Presently, she broke down and cried, tried to find a non-sore spot to hug, and finally got a welcoming smile from Joe.

Out in the waiting room, the man said, "I'm Frank, Joe's brother. I drove Amelia over here. And you are?"

"Radleigh Loonch, I've been working with Joe for awhile." Frank took the proffered hand. Rad waved at the two boys, "These fellows helped get Joe away from the thugs who were beating him." Ger gave a nod and a half wave. Kyle snored.

"Well, thanks for helping him. This isn't the first time he's taken a whipping. What was it about? He mess with some tough guy's girlfriend?"

"I don't think so—maybe just a mugging, I don't know. He was beaten badly, though."

Frank sighed and shrugged as if he'd been here before.

He saw the scene though the doors to the examining room and said, "Maybe now she will stop hating him so much. Is Dr. Bramton around?"

Rad pointed to a door behind Ger Blog and said, "Filling in some forms, I think."

"Well, thanks for your help. We'll take it from here. We'll get him home."

Mo saw red as he loped down the alley. Joe's enemies were his enemies and his blood was up, he was hot. There was no need to hunt for a trail. By coming up through a labyrinth of alleys, secluded parking areas and driveways, the "Arabs" had felt no need to disguise their escape route. They hadn't reckoned on Mo Snow. Nor would they have understood an "oppressed minority" fighting alongside his oppressor.

"No tail draggers here." Mo spoke to himself as he passed the discarded robes of Joe's assailants. He went down an alley that appeared, by the light from a yellow bug lamp high over a second-story window, to end in a blank wall. At the wall Mo saw that a gap between two buildings went to the right. It was a gap so narrow that Mo had to sidle through, his shoulders being too broad. The gap was thirty feet long and Mo slowed and looked as he neared the end. There, hidden behind downtown buildings, was a parking area sized for five cars. In that space, lit by a mercury vapor lamp, were two Mercedes Sedans heading in opposite directions.

Mo watched a heated conversation take place between one of the men he was chasing and someone in the back seat of the larger brown Mercedes. The language was unfamiliar to Mo. The car with the open window had a large Asian man in a suit beside each front door. These bodyguards were the ones Mo recognized from the mouth of the alley beside the House of Blues. He watched. The men argued. The Arab had his hand out. He wanted money. They appeared to feel safe where they were. Mo deduced that this lot must be on private property where they thought that they wouldn't be interrupted. A raven passed beneath the light, casting a shadow, and perched on a lintel. The men looked up. A second bird, the red-tailed hawk, crossed the light and perched on a disused crane that hung over a warehouse window on the building opposite. The "Arabs" were getting jumpy by the time the second bird arrived. The one who wasn't talking walked over and got in the passenger's side of the smaller Mercedes.

Mo closed his eyes. He had his helpers there and he formulated a plan. "It cannot happen until it is dreamed," he repeated this to himself three times as he reached in his pouch. Mo wore a small otter skin pouch on his belt and he carried some of his ceremonial items in the bag. Guns and knives were problematic when crossing borders and getting into and out of places, but a pouch with four stones the size of tennis balls and several sacred items was not denied. He called on his oyaron—power animal—ohkwari, the bear. His dream told him what to do.

Mo stepped from his hiding spot into the light. The raven croaked three times. The bodyguards looked up. The "Arab" leader looked up. The raven left his perch, flew in a circle creating a huge shadow, and returned to his perch. Moses X Snow wound up and threw a rock at the head of the passenger's side bodyguard, and seconds later, threw one into the parking lot light. There was a thwack like a rotten pumpkin hitting the sidewalk. Then a splintering crash as the light went out. The alley was plunged into darkness. The smaller car pealed out with a screech and headed down the alley to escape. Mo approached the larger Mercedes and drew a weapon from his ankle sheath.

The second car burned rubber to get out of the alley. With a burst of blitzing speed, Mo charged the bodyguard he had beaned. When the man wobbled to his feet trying to gain a fighting stance, he rubbed at his eyes to clear his vision. There was a loud crash at the mouth of the alley. The raven swooped down and tore at the bodyguard's head, flapped its wing before his eyes, blinding him further. Mo's weapon plunged into his throat and emptied his life. Walking swiftly down the alley, Mo saw the larger car, wrecked, its hood crumpled, steam geysering from the front. Moving left, away from the alley, a man and woman hurried away. The smaller car was gone. Mo slowly approached the wrecked Mercedes. In the driver's seat of the car sat the second huge bodyguard. His head lolled around as if he was barely conscious. In the back seat, a small Asian woman sat. She was wide-eyed in fear at the sight of Mo. He saw that she was stuck in the automobile.

Mo glanced at her, nodded, and yanked open the driver's door. He looked at the man, said one word of Mohawk—tsi hei—die, and plunged his weapon deep into the driver's throat. Mo then drew his hunting knife, reached up, flicked his blade neatly around the crown of the bodyguard's head and pulled the hair. With a pop, he took his ononrara, his scalp. Mo turned his gaze—calming now that he no longer saw the world tinted red—on the Asian woman.

"Don't kill me you crazy man, my foot is stuck under the seat in front. Did you do that? Did you make that huge bear stand up in front of the other car? Are you a sorcerer? The bear made the other car stop and we slammed into it so hard that I'm stuck here." Mo grinned at the thought of help from his asewandic—his dream talisman. He reached down and pushed the seat forward button and the girl gasped as the seat moved and she freed her foot.

"Don't kill me, I didn't do anything."

"Onen'ki'wahi," Mo said goodbye in Mohawk and turned back up the alleyway.

He removed the spirit head, scalp, from the first dead bodyguard, gathered up his throwing stones, honored his oyaron and left the parking lot by the back way.

Rad didn't know what to say. How much did this brother know? Should she talk to Joe's daughter? Anyway, she wasn't going to leave without at least one more word with Joe. She resumed her seat. The door opened and Agent Andre quietly stepped through looking so immaculately groomed Rad would have sworn it was five PM instead of nearly five AM.

"Gerhard, would you go down to the corner and get us some coffee and muffins please?" Ger's face lit up like a Christmas display. He moved quickly, snatched the offered twenty and Rad's keys and barreled through the door.

Alone with Rad, ignoring the snoring Kyle, Agent Andre asked to be filled in on some details. Rad hemmed and hawed, not knowing what to tell and what to omit.

"You have learned well from your mentor, Ms. Loonch. I'll make it easy for you, I will only ask a few questions to clarify my understanding."

"You were at the House of Blues, with Joe, just before the incident, correct?"

"Yes."

"The other two interns were with you, correct?"

"Yes."

"Joe left to meet Marv Ankara, at Ari Mantis's Neighborhood Place, but was assaulted in an alley off Benjamin Street, correct?"

Rad nodded, wondering what Agent Andre didn't know.

"You three, and some bystanders, were able to abort the attack and scare off the assailants, correct?"

"Yes,"- this more slowly. Rad noticed that he had left out Mo Snow, a distinctive person that witnesses must have mentioned.

"You don't know anything about any self-defense spray being used or how one assailant ended up dead, do you?"

"I didn't hit anyone, neither did Ger, and Kyle couldn't outwrestle a spaghetti noodle." Rad was gaining confidence now that the FBI Agent was not interested in *every* detail.

Agent Andre glanced at Kyle who moaned and lolled his head to the other side. He looked through to the examining room that now contained Dr. Bramton, Nurse Gruery, Frank, and Amelia all gathered around Joe. He was giving an, "Aw, shucks, it was nothing,'" speech.

Andre looked blandly at Rad.

"Do you want to know what the Pantherville police know?"

"Okay." Rad was a little unsure.

"They know that they have a dead person – a smalltime thug, well known to them, named Ali 'Al' Assad. He was the victim of violence, three separate injuries. From a baseball bat at the scene, CS gas, and contact with the alleyway asphalt."

"Since it was after midnight on Friday, they have no sober witnesses, to the death or any other activities. Channel #6 news is saying that a car fled the scene with an injured party. Witnesses say that a broken fence at a local nightspot was caused during the fight. There are also many fantastic reports of Arabs, Chinese Tong members, and screaming attacks by charging Indians. Everyone is sure, however, that this was not your usual Huron Street bar fight."

"How hard are the police going to investigate the death by violence of their old nemesis Al Assad? They won't be devoting too many officers or man-hours to this one, I don't think. A few more facts; no one got a reliable plate number or make and model off the car that removed the injured man. And though several inebriated witnesses said that they saw a hawk swoop through the alley twice, hawks don't fly at night. Perhaps it was an owl, a bird that flies at night."

Agent Andre looked at Rad in a way that combined a bland expressionless mouth with searching eyes. He was questioning and cautionary at the same time.

Rad squirmed under his gaze until the outer door swung open and Marv charged in. He was followed by Ger Blog with an enormous gallon sized coffee urn and a huge bag of muffins, bagels, and doughnuts.

Marv, seeing Joe behind the glass, headed right for him, ignored Rad, who he wasn't sure he liked, and Agent Andre, who he didn't know. Dr. Bramton and her nurse blocked his path and there was considerable loud talk and yelling for a few minutes until Joe spoke up, though it was obvious that his head hurt.

"Frank!" Joe winced. "Go get the car. Amelia, wait for me in the waiting room. Marie, let Marv through. Marv come here. Mr. Andre, I'll be with you in a minute."

Joe's hurting head caused him to lean to the left and squint his eyes tightly. When he opened his eyes, the people had been sorted out. Rad could hear the conversation through the open door to the examining room.

"Marv, you're a pain in the only place that doesn't already hurt, my ass."

"Joe, I'm sorry. Jackie B told me that Dumke was setting you up. But it was after I'd talked too much. I didn't know, Joe. I didn't know."

"It's ok Marv, they were already on my back trail."

"Are we still partners Joe? Are we?" Marv was blubbering like a drunk.

"Marv, go home. We'll fish this weekend, I'll be ok by then."

"I'll get that bastard Dumke, Joe, I'll kick his head in."

"No Marv, leave him be." Joe said. Agent Andre, who had quietly entered the room, nodded agreement.

"Mel Dumke will be left alone at this time, Marv. Do as Joe says. Go home, sleep it off." Marv sheepishly left the room, cowed by Andre's obvious authority, though unsure why he was obeying this little black guy. Andre closed the door. Joe and the FBI man had a conversation that Rad couldn't hear.

Rad and Amelia stepped out into the hall to get away from the sounds of slurping and lips smacking, and the listening ears of Ger and the awakened Kyle.

"What kind of trouble did you get my Dad in and who are all you people?"

Rad walked slowly along the corridor of closed offices, decided that she had to tell this young lady something, but struggled with how much detail she should provide. She knew that Amelia would have a hard time believing how little Rad actually knew about what Joe was up to.

"Men are almost exclusively performance oriented. They want to slay dragons, defend against charging lions, capture bad guys, and impress women with their heroism. Even when they do that, symbolically, they fear that it isn't enough. That metro-sexual man, in touch with his feelings, caring about his clothes, tender, and emotional, is BS created by Hollywood and Madison Avenue."

They stepped through the door into the August pre-dawn, cool, but foreshadowing a brilliant perfect late-summer day. There was a little bench. Rad sat and lit a cigarette. Amelia stood looking at her, unsure where the conversation was going.

"Your dad is a man of action. He believes that your mother hates him for being a screw-up and a failure. His great regret is that your love and respect is already lost to him. He fears that all your younger sisters will similarly be lost to him, one by one."

"How do you know all this? Who are you?" This last sentence came with the emphasis on the middle word. Hands on hips, face squeezed tight, Amelia was challenging and begging at the same time

"My name is Radleigh Loonch, I work for the Department of Homeland Security, specifically, what you would call the Border Patrol. I've been working with Joe since mid May." The six years difference in ages between these young women, Rad, 23, and Amelia, 17, was enough to move the younger one inexorably toward a position of respect and awe toward the older one. Amelia sat on the bench, asked for a cigarette, and awkwardly lit up.

"My little sisters worship Dad. They don't even know about losing the jobs, the DUIs or his other screw-ups."

"I can't say much about his present job—in fact I don't know that much—but he is trying to make something of himself because of that other baggage. He is all man, your dad."

"You're saying that he hasn't been going to a big construction project in Pantherville with that loser Marv every day? He's working for the Feds, he's fighting terrorism."

"Marv drops him at a Park and Ride every day and I pick him up and he is based out of Pantherville, though we get around a bit."

"Does my Mom know this?"

"She knows some of it. I've met your Mother, once. I don't know what he has told her but he probably thought it best for security and your family's safety to keep everyone out of the loop as much as possible."

"You're serious aren't you?"

"Very much so. You should definitely keep this from the younger children and tell no one at school or anywhere else. I expect you'll talk this over with your Mom. I do know that he loves you and your Mother very much, but, like a man, he can't figure out any way to show it. Or, I guess, it is more accurate to say, he doesn't give himself credit for the ways he shows his love."

"Why doesn't he just talk to us or include us in the stuff he does?"

"I'm afraid that idea never occurs to a man."

Frank came out through the door holding a coffee cup in one hand and a doughnut in the other. He walked up to Amelia, ignoring Rad and said, "I'm gonna pull around to the side door." He gestured with his doughnut, "Get your dad and help him out that door. And Amy, grab a couple doughnuts or muffins on the way through, you know what an appetite he has."

She got up to go back into the clinic and turned to Rad, "Thank you, Ms. Loonch, it was a pleasure to meet you." They shook hands in that way women do where they seem to barely touch each other.

Agent Andre came out the door and approached Rad. "I have an errand to run in Coleman. Joe is going to take a few days off. You three interns should report to your agencies. I'll contact you as to when you should begin meeting Joe at the Park and Ride again." The Agent brushed a crumb from his sleeve and said his polite goodbye. Before he walked to his car he said, "The Bureau has in custody the bodies of two stout Asian gentlemen, suspected of being agents of the People's Liberation Army. These are persons of interest in the death of Derek Chang."

"How'd that happen, were these guys in the alley?"

"We work problems from more than one angle. By the way, we have never had this conversation."

Rad sat down and finished her cigarette. She was completely baffled by everyone. Joe went home, helped out the side door by Frank and Amelia. Rad was left to drive back to Pantherville, with the rising sun behind her. Ger and Kyle snored in their seats.

Marv Ankara

Chapter 17

September 4th

The two busiest weekends of the boating season on the Musky Straits are Independence Day weekend and Labor Day weekend. It seems everyone in a boat is flying around at those times. Labor Day is busier for two reasons: it is the beginning of the end for warm weather boaters and the last gaspers are all out, and it is a holiday for both Canadians and Americans. The Straits were packed with traffic. All the big booze cruisers would go down the Strait early and come back late. Fishermen, jet skiers, sailors, and water skiers were out in force. There was a huge poker run planned, wherein the speed boaters rushed from here to there, picking up playing cards at each stop, while trying to outrace everyone in their class and have the best poker hand. The noise from the passing boats on a poker run rivaled that from an airport runway.

Labor Day Monday was the pinnacle of this activity and Joe had not planned to be on the Straits. He had a family picnic scheduled in Muskedaigua and was trying, as always, to mend some fences with his wife and daughters. It was a phone call Sunday night from Jackie B and the warning from Andre's Yemeni informants that got him thinking, and his dream that convinced him that he'd heard enough to expect something big on Labor Day.

Jackie said that Mel Dumke had been in his cups at the beer tap and bragged about how he'd not want to be on the Friendship Bridge on Monday. Jackie had walked past to go to his back room when Mel was telling Johnny Lawrence this. Johnny assumed he was talking about the inevitable traffic jam as all the cottagers came back from the Canadian beaches at the end of the weekend and the summer. Jackie had paused while headed back to the shop with some supplies. He heard Dumke say "Boom!" and wave his hands in the air shaking his fingers like debris raining down. Dumke then let loose with a cackling laugh.

Jackie was not the only one who had called Joe on Sunday night. He also heard from Johnny Lawrence about the same conversation. Johnny had been feeding Joe information all summer, though it usually was a little late to be of use. The third phone call was the clincher. It was from the other Melvin, Mel Loonch. He told Joe that he'd been talking with Ian Drakulitch on Friday and Ian had been remarking about Mel Dumke consulting with him to buy two boats. Ian barked a derisive laugh because Dumke had proceeded to buy two Coastliners for a client, despite Ian's strong advice to the contrary.

"He only cared about the size of the cabin on that thirty-two footer," Ian had said, "and when I asked what his clients were hauling, he'd said, 'I don't care what those Sand Niggers haul in their boats.' He was going to be in Pennsylvania on Monday."

It was Joe's dream on Sunday night that pulled these threads together. He was helping his wife mix the potato salad Monday morning when he remembered that dream and the spirit bear telling him that he must stop this. At 10:30 AM he got on the phone to his contact in the Coast Guard. After ten rings a bored female voice answered. She wouldn't or couldn't find out where anyone was and Joe left a message for Delmar Norris.

"He'll call you back right away."

"Yeah, right," said Joe, and he tried the Army Corps of Engineers, the guys in charge of the infrastructure. They must be interested in a threat to the bridge. There, the phone was answered by a voice mail system that sent one down several different paths depending on the options chosen. Unless one knew the extension of one's party—Joe didn't—all the voice mail menus led to a disconnection. It was now 11:45 and he didn't know where to go next.

He was ready to call Rad when he discovered a card in his wallet that had an 800 number to call in case of an imminent threat. Joe tried it. He got answered on the first ring.

"This is Joe Gaspe, I have uncovered a plot to sabotage the Friendship Bridge by ramming it with a boat full of explosives."

"Excuse me sir could you give me your service number, I must verify this information."

"I haven't got any service number. I'm calling to alert you to an emergency. They're going to blow up the Friendship Bridge! Right now! Today!"

"That bridge is located in what state, sir?" Joe noticed the pronounced accent of this operator for the first time. He began to wonder if the person he was talking to was even an American.

"Where is this number I'm calling?"

"This line rings through to Washington DC, sir."

"But where are you?"

"My location is of no concern to you; I assure you, sir, I have a direct link…"

"You're not even in the USA are you?" Joe had had enough. He hung up.

His next call was to Rad. "Can you get hold of Agent Andre and meet me at the marina? It's urgent." Rad was doing nothing special on Labor Day, she told her dad not to cook her steak and agreed to meet Joe.

It was two fifteen PM by the time Joe and Rad had met, opened the boathouse, warmed up the motors, and eased the Whaler into the channel. There was traffic everywhere. There was a line to buy gas at the Royal Marina pumps. There were boats idling waiting for the lock to open so they could move up to the lake. The lock was also full of down-bound boats that would be added to the crush. The boats were of all sizes, from kayaks to forty-five footers. The right of way to boat traffic in the Straits was controlled by the big boats, according to the rules of the road. On a busy holiday, like Labor Day, cruisers thirty feet long and longer owned the waterway.

The rules of the road state that the less maneuverable boat has the right of way over the more maneuverable boat when it comes to motorized craft. The effect of this is that, "The biggest dog whips," as Joe Gaspe put it. Therefore the boat that caused the largest disturbance in traffic and threw the biggest wake could fly through the traffic pattern, unconcerned about anyone else. To complicate matters, not every big cruiser was being driven by someone who could judge the relative size of different boats. At mid-afternoon, quite a few mimosas, bloody marys, and brewskies had been consumed. It was chaos.

A twenty-foot boat like the Whaler had no priority and had to give way constantly to other boats. There were three to five foot waves in the Straits created by the wakes of those cruisers going up and down channel. Traffic following the channel had priority over traffic moving cross channel. Joe and Rad waited, idling and bobbing on the waves, like concertgoers trying to enter the main aisle as a packed house emptied. Joe was nervous, his stomach was churning with worry, and he wanted Rad to take the wheel while he worked the radio trying to rouse the Coast Guard, the County Sheriff, somebody. Rad was not about to try driving in that mess since about one-third of the boat drivers either didn't know the rules of the road, or didn't care. People were cutting in, flying around, honking at each other, shaking fists, and cussing streams of expletives, inaudible to anyone but those on their own boat.

Joe didn't want to talk on the emergency channel of the VHF radio, channel sixteen, or the alternate emergency channel, number nine, because he thought the bad guys might be listening on them. But he did tune to sixteen to hear the chaos of several boats, dead in the water, out of gas, or involved in collisions with injury. After one minute of listening on sixteen he dropped down to nine. It was just as chaotic, and Joe realized why he'd been unable to get any attention from the Coast Guard—their plate was full to overflowing. One of their patrol boats was involved with a boat that had piled up on the water intake down the strait. They were trying to rescue children in the water. The other patrol boat was up in the lake dealing with a multi-vessel collision. A cruiser had smashed up three jet skis as if they were bowling pins. Joe concluded that there was nothing for it but to try to intercept the bomb vessel himself. Joe's judgment was not always good, but when he decided he was right he went ahead, vigorously.

Taking the wheel back from Rad, he said, "Call Andre again. Leave a message telling him I'm going to stop an attempt to bomb the Friendship Bridge. Leave a message for Commander Norris telling him the same thing, use your name or mine. After that, use the binoculars to start looking for a thirty-two-foot Coastliner driving strangely. We're going to intercept it." Joe boldly pulled into traffic, earning himself curses from a nineteen foot Sea Ray driven by a shirtless man burned as red as a cooked lobster.

Bobbing from side to side in an arc thirty degrees off vertical, Rad saw likely boats all over the Straits. She didn't know how to tell a Coastliner from any other boat. The noise was deafening. The look on Joe's face, and the firm yet calm way he handled his boat, was not like anything she'd seen from him before. She respected him for his composure in the confusion around him. She was scared, too scared to get seasick. She leaned over and yelled to Joe, "I don't know what we're looking for."

"Eliminate all the down-bound traffic, they're past the Bridge. Any big boats you suspect, point them out to me!" He shouted and grinned at her, winked, and added, "Now we're going to earn our bread!"

Rad muttered to herself, "Can I take a voluntary layoff?"

Joe's driving was impeccable as he passed slower traffic, bounced over the wakes of bigger boats, and weaved his way south down the Straits heading for the bridge. The act of crossing a three-foot wake at twenty-five miles per hour took the Whaler airborne repeatedly. It would smash the water with a shuddering slam and a soaking spray of water. After the smack of crossing a big wake, Joe would jerk the wheel into the calmer water in the trough of the wake and head onward. It was four miles from where they entered the Straits to the narrows where the Friendship Bridge had been built in 1928. Being a narrow part of the Straits, where the millions of acre-feet of water from the Upper Lake poured down a funnel headed for the Musky Falls, the water under the bridge had the fastest current in the Straits, save that at the brink of the falls. No boat lolled around under the bridge. They moved at speed up bound to the lake or down-bound into the Straits. On Labor Day the narrows rolled with boat wakes that rebounded off both shores and held a constant churning mass of six to eight foot waves. These waves didn't bother the big cruisers much, but played hell with smaller craft such as Joe's Boston Whaler.

The true believers picked for their mission, unsophisticated and trusting, knew very little about how to drive a thirty-two foot boat. Hassan, the pilot, had an Ontario driver's license but he had had only four hours of instruction in driving a boat. He had no feeling for how a boat steers from the back. One familiar with driving a car needed to react as if one was seated on the hood of the car looking backwards and driving in reverse in order to understand how a boat would respond to the helm. In addition, Hassan had no understanding of the profound effect friction has on a boat. Since the entire bottom is experiencing drag, a boat thrown into neutral slows very rapidly and begins to wallow, immediately. Also, the flow of the water, current, and wind move the boat even when it is under power.

The wisdom of making this test run in the thirty-two foot Coastliner became apparent when Hassan tried to weave his way through Labor Day traffic while Tariq used a digital stopwatch and a tachometer to judge speed and timing. He needed to find out how close they could get to the bridge so the timer could be set for detonation.

Joe and Rad were halfway between the Railroad Bridge and the Friendship Bridge, with Joe concentrating on getting past a twenty-five foot Wellcraft, when Rad leaned over and yelled, "What is that?" She was looking at the central arch of the bridge and pointing.

"There it is. We're too late!" Joe yelled veering to port and dropping his throttles into idle. Joe, expecting an explosion, no longer saw a need to proceed into what would become the blast area. He and Rad watched as several larger boats continued on their up bound courses straight for the arch. The voice traffic on channel sixteen increased with many people trying to call the Coast Guard and transmissions from open mikes stepping all over each other.

Joe was sure that the down bound Coastliner was one of the ones Dumke purchased. He was sick with horror watching the impending destruction of the bridge and its many occupied vehicles. Rad, who didn't know exactly what she was watching, picked up on Joe's tension and, hearing his stream of curse words, added a few of her own. Joe squeezed the steering wheel with white hands. Rad stood behind him with her brow wrinkled and her lower lip protruding. They were furious with the oncoming boat but could do nothing to change the feared results.

Then, coming through clearly on Channel Sixteen of the VHF, "Down-bound Coastliner, give way. This is up-bound Trojan, Sandblaster, give way, you idiot." This was shouted while the pilot of the Trojan laid on the horn. Joe stared through the center arch of the Friendship Bridge.

The boat that he was sure was a floating bomb had just veered from hitting an up-bound Trojan 37 at the last second before collision. The Trojan, stubborn to a fault, never gave way to the smaller vessel. The Coastliner had narrowly missed the bridge and spun down-stream in a dead stall, turning one full circle in the back eddy, before slowly drifting down the Canadian side of the Straits. Several other vessels had to juke and jive to miss the seemingly derelict Coastliner. Many of these boats tried to contact the Coast Guard to report the reckless pilot of the Coastliner. While drifting down the Canadian side, the pilot restarted the Coastliner. He got underway, going back the way he had come, and went under the bridge, turned to starboard and motored into the Ontario waters of the Upper Lake.

"It was a trial run, that's your boat over in Ontario," Rad said.

"Let's go home." Joe turned downstream and headed back to the marina. He passed a Sheriff's boat, blue light flashing, heading towards the near collision. The Musky County Sheriff was powerless to ticket or even interview a Canadian vessel. Joe had an ominous feeling, but there had been no explosion so his prediction was wrong. "That will have consequences," Joe thought.

"There's nothing they can do, the whole thing happened in Canada," Joe said to Rad. He wondered if his warnings would give him a reputation for crying wolf.

Five days later Rad was finally going musky fishing with Joe and Marv. Joe wanted her and Marv to get along. He knew Marv was jealous of her and did not want that to continue. He worried that she would be bored, though he knew she had musky fished with her father in years past.

"Let's see how many different species of birds we can see as the day goes on. I bet it will be at least twenty."

Joe said this as they backed out of the boathouse slowly, and then drove out through the no-wake zone around the marina.

"Ducks, geese, terns, gulls, pigeons, and sparrows so far." Rad accepted the diversion of bird watching.

"We're going to try a run your father showed me. A run that can produce numbers, though rarely does it give up a big one.' Joe said this before he advanced his twin throttles, ramped the Whaler up to thirty mile per hour, and headed down the Straits in the direction of Musky Falls.

Twenty minutes later they were trolling downstream. Rad was driving, Marv monitoring their lines, and Joe explaining his pattern.

"We're trolling a twenty-four foot flat with little bottom variation. We are bouncing the bottom with deep diving crank baits, using one hundred feet of braided Spectra line. A small rise of a foot or two will cause the lure to crash hard against the bottom. When the lure starts to jump and bounce, that's when the musky hits."

Marv piped up, "They follow the lures and attack when the rhythm changes."

"Um-hmm, egret, green heron, osprey, and of course cormorant." Rad was listening, but bird watching as well.

"Cormorants! I hate cormorants! They should all be killed! I say we should have a year round hunting season, no limit on cormorants!" This was a subject that animated Marv. Joe's face broke into a grin and he winked at Rad.

"So you'd have idiots shooting shotguns all over the place." Joe was goading Marv, just for fun. Suddenly, a reel clicker began to scream.

"Fish on! Neutral! Joe, get that other line in!" Marv was fired up now.

Joe was reeling in the other line when he said, "Marv give the rod to our guest. She's up."

"You're fishing the rotation? That's bull!" Nevertheless, Marv handed Rad the rod and helped Joe ready the boat for landing a fish. Rad kept the rod tip high, no pumping required, and reeled like mad as the musky used one of the species' favorite tricks and ran straight at the boat. This would create slack in the line and, if the fish leaped with a slack line, it could get free.

While trolling downstream the caught fish is forced to fight the rod and reel as well as the effect of current on a heavy boat. If not landed quickly, the fish can be exhausted to the point of death. When all the muscles in her body get loaded with lactic acid and become oxygen deprived, she can die.

Rad's musky was not large—around thirty-six inches—and she did a fine job bringing her right to boatside. Marv was ready to handle her and, after an in-water picture, reached down with his needle nosed pliers and yanked the one hook from her mouth. The musky calmly swam away.

The musky run that they were fishing has a history of nests of fish. That is, if you caught one in a spot, it was wise to go right back over the same spot, immediately. More fish could very often follow.

"Musky Bill says, 'If it works do it again.'" Joe directed Rad to rerun the same area.

In this way they were able to land three more fish in the next two hours. Marv ended up with the largest musky. Joe got a nice one and Rad caught two muskies on one outing for the first time in seven years.

The fishing was not easy, however, because the water was still infested with jet-skis and the lines became clogged with weeds continually. After four hours, the wakes caused by large boats cruising the Straits forced them to abandon their run.

Just before they headed south toward the marina, Rad asked, "Could that be an eagle?"

Joe said, "A golden eagle is rarer than a bald eagle. But you might be right."

The run up to the area near the marina was uneventful and Joe suggested that they run across the current a few times before quitting for the day.

The first pass towards Frog Creek, short lining shallow diving baits, turned up nothing but weeds. After a turn at the Canadian side, Joe slowed down as a boat came alongside. Rad recognized Mo Snow standing in the stern of the other boat and she waved at him. Mo gestured with open arms to Rad and Joe. The cousins communicated without words as the boats idled along side by side. A great blue heron slowly flapped its wings above the two boats, easily besting the wind.

A red tailed hawk crossed perpendicular to them and made its signature call, ker, ker, ker.

"You know those two guys that set me up for the beating?"

"Yeah…" Rad said that with a dubious expression.

"Mo got 'em."

"How do you know that?" Marv asked.

"He told me." Joe said this with a twinkling eye and a slight grin. No words had passed, but Joe knew.

Chapter 18

September 12th

U ncle Mike reached out and touched each of his four pipes to find the coolest one for his next smoke. He was listening to Joe Gaspe and didn't break eye contact with him while he selected an old-fashioned corncob pipe, packed it with a mixture of commercial and native tobacco, and lit a "strike anywhere" kitchen match. Joe continued to talk with the sucking wheezing sound of a pipe smoker in the background.

"Sometimes it takes me a year to get my mind around an idea. I need to work on it and put it to the back of my mind and bring it up later and work it some more. I've got a partner, Rudyard, who breaks down ideas in nothing flat; he's probably not always right, but he is always sure of himself. He likes to say he's already done the reading for me. But it's not his philosophies that I need to ask you about. It's these dreams that I've been having. Mainly, there are three dreams that keep recurring. I dream a lot of dreams and since you've showed me how, I can remember them. But, three come back again and again. One of travel, one of warning, and one is just a piece of a dream, really just a scene. I haven't talked about them—honored them as you would say—to anyone yet and, and, well, I don't know…"

Uncle Mike looked at Joe with an impassive face, but his eyes showed concern, interest, suspense, and satisfaction. They were in his smoking room, hardly larger than a walk-in closet. It contained a small pot-bellied stove, a kitchen table, a beat-up armchair, and three mismatched kitchen chairs. The walls were hung with ceremonial calumets. They could have been authentic or reproductions, Joe couldn't tell. There was a painted slate leaning on a top shelf and it had a stylized wolf on it. There was a pipe rack, ashtray, and coffee pot with two cups on the table. Beside his chair Uncle Mike kept a pile of fishing and hunting magazines that were well-thumbed and out-of-date, having been culled from waiting rooms.

Joe felt guilty about asking Rad to bring him down to Uncle Mike's cabin on the Rez and then asking her to stay in the car at the bottom of the hill. He wanted to speak privately with the sachem and not do any more explaining than necessary.

Several minutes passed while Uncle Mike made sure that Joe was finished talking. He puffed on his pipe. Joe smoked a cigarette. Each sipped coffee.

"Tell me the dream of travel."

Joe told of his journey as a hawk, following a raven to a far off wild jungle land.

The old man said softly, "Yo-hay," made a chopping motion, and bade Joe to continue.

When Joe mentioned the arrival of Mo Snow as the heron, he heard another, "Yo-hay."

Uncle Mike sat quietly and stared at the Coleman lantern during Joe's explanation of the frogs, newts, and efts and their transformation in his mind to the faces of evil people both known, like Mel Dumke, and unknown and unfamiliar. Joe caught his breath, lit another cigarette, looked at Uncle Mike staring into the lantern, stared at the tip of the flame himself, and stated, "These are the faces of evil, my enemies, aren't they?"

"Yo-hay, these are enemies to you. The dark twin is revealing himself to you. Has this dream showed itself in the shadow world yet?"

"No, but I've seen Dumke and interacted with him. Nothing special, though."

"Tell me of the small section of a dream that you mentioned."

"There isn't much to tell. I pass two silver coins or medals stacked but about to slide onto the floor. I stop, straighten the stack, stop it from falling, and go on my way. I am always going somewhere and the coins are in passing."

"These medals, describe them, please."

"I don't really see them in the dream but I first thought that they were Franklin half dollars, you know, the old kind. Now, I see them as bigger than half dollars, bigger than silver dollars. They are silver with an ugly white man on them and Franklin is in the background encouraging me to take care that the medals are not separated. It's a very short dream but it happens a lot. Is this important?"

Mike chopped the air softly, "Yo-hay."

They sat for a few moments each looking at the Coleman lantern. Joe broke the silence by asking, "Should I tell you of the warnings?"

Uncle Mike looked up, startled. He frowned, returned his gaze to the lantern, puffed his pipe, blew out a cloud of smoke, sighed, and said, "Please, do."

Joe told of his dream, and he emphasized the vividness and physically exhausting nature of this vision. When he mentioned the heron and the bear, the old man said, "Yo-hay," each time. Joe sat back and said after a short pause, "I can smell the burning sulfur after that dream is over."

"You were correct to bring these to me. Without dream seers, around the council fires, you young people have difficulty honoring your dreams. You must find someone to whom you can tell these dreams and who can help you see the events that are in store for you after the dreaming."

"I'm not so young, grandfather. What do they mean? Is there someone near my home I can tell my dreams to? Can you tell me what will happen?"

Mike sighed, appeared annoyed at Joe's impatience, and busied himself refilling the cups of coffee. He took his time and said, "Yes." He laid his bony brown hand on the table, said, "Place your hand lightly over my wrist, close your eyes and dream with me."

Joe's eyes were smarting from the smoky room. He did as he was told. He saw right away that the raven looked like Uncle Mike and was leading him, the hawk, on another flight. As they ascended, Joe saw his cousin, Mo Snow, who was the heron, swooping through the dream. When all three birds perched in front of a cave on a high cliff face, Joe looked deep into the cave and saw his daughter Amelia beckoning. Joe said, "Amy!?!?" and lifted his hand. His eyes shot open and Uncle Mike's did as well.

The sachem let a few minutes pass while Joe absorbed the power of the moment. "Did you see?"

"I was with you, Joe. I saw. Your travel dreams tell you that I am with you on your discoveries and that Moses Snow is with you too. He is the heron. The warning is coming through your oyaron, your spirit guide, the bear. The medals are the symbols of unity in the Mohawk longhouse. At the Congress of Albany, one was given to the people of Kahnawake and one to the people of the Upper Castle. They were to forever remind us that we are brothers, not to make war on each other, and that our Six Nations could unite all the people. Your daughter, grandchild of a woman of power, has the gift of dreaming and medicine skills. Let her tell you her dreams and you tell her those that you must honor. You will know the dreams that need to be honored."

"Amy is the one who should listen? "

"The people of the longhouse have always been led by our wise women. They have chosen the war chiefs and the sachems and they have removed them when necessary. Always there were special women, women of power. These were healers who could see the medicines in the forest and they were power dreamers. Power dreamers dream true, but they also see the long view. Dreaming was important for warriors and hunters, but the warrior gets his blood up and cannot see the future if it is many looks away. The woman of power sees this, she visits the real world and knows all that has happened and that will happen. Your mother was a woman of power who was gone from this life too soon. She had no daughters so it falls to one of her granddaughters to accept this responsibility. It is your daughter, Amelia, who will carry on the tradition of Island Woman."

Uncle Mike stopped and Joe nodded in a hesitant manner. Mike continued, "You must help Amelia understand her power. Her grandmother helps her but the girl needs to be reassured. The white world will tell her she has dropped her mind. You, Joe, must honor her dreams with her and let her know how a woman of power must live. She will also learn, from her grandmother, that she can honor your dreams."

"Okay, one last question. The bear growls and snorts in the dream, but I hear it as if it speaks English. Is that right?"

"Yo-hay."

The early fall twilight had faded in the Allegheny Mountains when Joe sat back, looked at Uncle Mike, and felt the tension drain from his neck and shoulders. He was calm. He knew what was to happen. His coffee cup was empty, he was out of cigarettes, and he had a long walk through the dark to descend the mountain to where Rad was parked in her Malibu.

"Time to get going." Uncle Mike stared straight ahead.

"Man! I had to get outta there." Marv said this as he plopped into a chair on the deck outside of Joe's kitchen.

"The fumes got to us tonight." Joe said this with a chuckle. He referred to the glue used to lay up the split bamboo sections of his custom fly rods. The rod they had been working on this night was a four-piece pack rod he'd been making for Agent Andre. The split pieces of the top section, the thinnest section, were exceedingly small. Joe's fingers, heavy, blunt, fat like sausages, failed him on this job. His partner, Marv, was proud to be able to help on this close work.

"The glue fumes weren't as bad as Tony's mud butt. That was bad!" Marv referred to Tony Gill, a friend who'd been around to visit.

"He was gassy—the shop is too small to be able to get away from that smell. Do you suppose he noticed how we both ran to the opposite corner each time he fumed?" Marv laughed, and Joe looked up to see his daughter Amy and her best friend Randi DesChutes looking at them.

"Eeyoo, don't boys ever stop laughing about farts?"

"Amy, you and I have to talk. Hi, Randi. Stay here and keep Marv company for a few minutes." Joe led Amelia inside. Marv nodded at Randi and said nothing.

Amy was worried. Had a note come from school? Had somebody's parents called? Whenever her Dad wanted to talk, it was never anything good. They sat at the kitchen table.

"Daughter, have I ever told you about Uncle Mike, the Seneca sachem I go to see once in awhile?"

"No." That one syllable lay there as a statement and a question.

"Well, one day we'll go see him. But right now, I'm going to explain something a little complicated, so hear me out. Your grandmother, who died when I was very young, was a special woman of the Iroquois. She was what they call a power dreamer. That's a woman who was meant to be a leader of the clan and the tribe. She carried on a traditional role that has always been inherited from mother to daughter. But she had no daughters, only seven sons. In that case the power to dream true would go to one of her granddaughters. Uncle Mike told me yesterday that that is you." Joe had been talking fast, afraid she would interrupt.

Instead of interrupting, or being skeptical, her favorite phrase was, "no way," Amy nodded. This was what was happening to her. She was possessed in a way.

Joe continued. "Uncle Mike says that the big problem with the men of the Six Nations, who are no longer warriors and don't hunt much either, is that they have lost the dreaming. Without the dreaming they have no explanation of what to do with their lives. This is why so many of us drink and take pills, and sniff gasoline, and get hooked on meth. We are nowhere and don't know who we are, and we don't know what to do. But the thing is, Uncle Mike says, those of us who dream, we've got to honor our dreams, not try to forget them, but tell them to each other, and try to understand what they mean. Does this make any sense?"

Amy said, "Well, I guess. I mean I've been having these dreams, and not just when I'm asleep. But, you're my dad. There's stuff I won't be telling you."

"All of your dreams don't have to be honored. You and I will do a little work on this. Uncle Mike says that we'll know the ones that need work."

"I have been having very intense dreams with an Indian woman who looks sort of like your stepmother, grandmother's sister."

"Those are the ones you must tell me. I will have some to tell you as well."

"I'll think about it." Amelia was at an age where she was skeptical about her dad.

"You do that. We'll talk more."

"We've got the best part of the day awaiting us," Joe sounded more optimistic than he felt. He would have rather gone fishing but Marv had met a lady with whom he wanted to cruise. He'd even found one with a girlfriend for Joe. They'd waited out the thunderstorms in a local watering hole. Thankfully, it wasn't a sports bar, a ubiquitous type of tavern overloaded with monstrous televisions and loud yelling boys who were obsessed with the spectacle of professional sports. With baseball in full swing, there would be a different game on each TV. Joe hated sports bars and Marv didn't care, as he was always on the hunt for women and there were better prospects at non-sports bars.

Marv had scored, in his mind anyway, with a shapely woman who had the same thing on her mind, after several drinks, as him. She was attractive, but had a hard look in her face and eyes that suggested to Joe that she wanted to use Marv as he intended to use her. Marv was unmarried and free to dock in any slip he chose. Joe, a married father of five, wasn't going to fool himself. Though he wasn't morally opposed to a roll with a comfort woman, he wasn't that good of a man, he had to be tempted more than he was now by Nicole. She was a friendly girl who seemed to know what she was in for, but her relentless talk, about herself, grated on Joe's nerves. He tried to imagine a knockout supermodel, and then she giggled, talked of her likes and dislikes, and ended the fantasy.

Oh well, Marv was well along toward his goal, and they had food and drink, maybe Joe's enthusiasm would increase as they cruised the

Straits. Joe had left home in a snit, feeling unappreciated because of his intermittent sex life. He had told himself that he could do with something strange. "Marv, never live in a house with more than one adult women," he'd said on the drive to Pantherville. "They'll synchronize their periods and all of them will be crabby and bitchy for the same week each month."

"All three? At the same time?" Marv's sympathy was genuine, if not deeply felt.

"Three now and another in a year or two. It's a pity I can't afford to send 'em away to college as they reach the age, but they'll be living at home the whole time."

"Maybe Katie will throw you out." Marv said that with a conspiratorial laugh.

"Could happen, Marv, could definitely happen."

All men felt some self-pity when they were not esteemed enough, in their minds, and like most, Joe knew it was a pathetic and weak way to think. That didn't stop him though, because there was pleasure in feeling justified when being a jerk. He was well into his huff when they reached Gianni's, the bar where Marv thought he could find Christina. Marv was right. Now it was up to Joe to entertain Nicole while Marv and his date went below, to the cuddy cabin, and got down to business. There was rustling below as Marv moved aside fishing rods, tackle boxes, rain gear, and such to make room for two active adults.

"If it's rockin' don't be knockin'," said Marv as he closed the hatch with a hearty laugh.

There was a giggle and a slap from down below. Marv seemed to be making progress toward his goal. Joe tried to drive the boat while his date worked hard with her hands and lips vying for his attention. In between discourse on her hair, her diet, her sisters, her shopping, and her preferences, Nicole was progressing toward that situation where she hoped Joe would make his move. At least, that was how he was interpreting the signals, with a man's overconfidence and overzealousness.

The Whaler was in US waters and cocktails were allowed. One didn't have to boat under the influence to get in trouble in Ontario, having booze aboard was sufficient to be fined heavily. Joe had one short line fishing rod trolling behind the boat. If his wife asked, he could honestly say he'd been fishing. Zigzagging down current toward a cloudy sky he called Nicole's attention to the clouds moving off to the northeast. They were shaded from white through blue to slate to gray to charcoal to the farthest north ones, that were the black thunderheads from the earlier storms. While Joe and Nicole watched, the setting sun, knifing through the clearing western sky, turned the clouds every shade of red, as if a giant's hand had dragged a paintbrush across the sky.

Joe turned down the radio, interrupted Marv's unh,unh,unh, to bellow, "Look at the clouds, Marv. This is worth seeing. Look out the window." Joe recranked the volume.

Nicole was citing the reds that she saw as color swept across the formerly gray skies turning each different cloud color a distinctive red, "Pink, coral, rose, red, strawberry, crimson, scarlet, maroon, peach, cranberry, fuchsia, this is magical, Joe."

"Fuchsia? I don't know fuchsia." Joe was worried now.

"Magic, Joe, it is like the sky is on fire. And look at that ship— it's on fire too!" she squealed with delight pointing at the glass-walled cruise ship. Its windows reflected the red sky as the setting sun glinted across it.

"A Fireship, huh?" Joe felt as if his mind would explode. This was an astounding sight, but he was getting into something he really didn't want to be in, and he heard the voice of one of his mentors, Rudyard Loonch saying, "The old time sailors spoke of more than one kind of Fireship, Joe. Sometimes, the fireships were in port. Every port had its fireships."

Now Joe's only thought was to get out of this situation without interrupting Marv or hurting the feelings of the willing young lady who was practically on his lap. She wasn't so bad. Perhaps at another time, another place. But what to tell her?

"Nicole, I'm married. More or less happily married."

"You don't think I've done a married man before?" She was getting annoyed now and the magical moment had gone. The sun finished setting. The red colors disappeared.

"It's not you, it's me. I just don't feel right." He was annoyed by her, but not irritated as he'd be with a beautiful woman or one he cared about. A woman who moved him emotionally could be endlessly irritating, because he cared. A woman he didn't care about just annoyed him when she got nasty. Her feelings were hurt by rejection. Joe, like most men, had experienced rejection many times and his attitude was to forget it and look for the next opportunity.

When they returned the boat to the boathouse, they'd caught no fish.

Financial shenanigans were one of those subjects that mystified Joe Gaspe and resulted in a sick headache that took days to overcome. He had insisted that Radleigh come along to the CPO's Club for his meeting with Bill Cote because, as a college girl, she'd understand better and, as a second listener, she'd remember better than Joe. It didn't help that much, since she affected a girl's insouciance about finances and displayed a lil' ole' me attitude toward the subject.

It didn't help Joe's understanding when Cote repeated everything three times and went off on tangents about his personal finances with alarming frequency.

"I use coupons at as many stores as are in my neighborhood. I see no way Colgate Palmolive can make money, with manufacturers' coupons for a dollar off, two-for-one sales, and store coupons. I get my toothpaste, toilet tissue and soap for the sales tax."

"How much toothpaste do you need?" Joe was inadvertently encouraging him while Rad rolled her eyes, already tired of this noise.

"If you watch and use the coupon when they are out of stock, they'll give you a rain check. With the rain check, you just go in and take the product. You don't even have to pay the sales tax then, don't you know."

"What's this got to do with Mel Dumke's $50 bill?" Rad wanted to move on, even though Cote was buying the drinks. He was so annoying that he dried up her thirst.

"I was helping out as a forensic accountant after the fall of Saddam. You remember that several caches of US currency were discovered on the property of his associates?" Cote was back on point.

"Yeah, I saw that on Fox news," Rad said.

"Well, the majority of that cash was turned over to the new Iraqi government eventually, but a portion was arranged to be stolen and put into the hands of terrorists."

"What? We let them have US cash?" Joe couldn't stop the pounding in his temples.

"Not before we tagged it. You see, we wanted to see where it would turn up—in whose hands—so we marked it with a radio tag. I don't understand the technology but apparently the geeks can pick up a signal off those bills and find them in a limited radius. Engineers are amazing these days."

"The fifty that Dumke gave Joe came from the Iraq stash?" Rad was catching on faster than Joe, who was still thinking about the toothpaste caper. "But I thought it was the Chinese who were smuggling the people in from Canada?"

"That money, or money from the same cache, I should say, has also showed up on one of the dead Chinese bodyguards found at the downtown building where they were killed. The limo was rented with more of it."

"A cache of cash. I think I'm gonna be sick." Joe was starting to see the absurdity here.

"The Chicoms have been paid a lot of money from the terrorists in Iraq, here in Pantherville? Are they financing the alien smuggling? Or are they paying to have their own assets brought in? What does Andre say?" Rad needed to create order in her mind about this.

"Agent Andre does not confide in me, but I think he believes that the Chinese who smuggle the aliens are doing other jobs for Al Qaeda and being paid in cash. US dollars are useful anywhere for anything. I think he considers it likely that they smuggle aliens, drugs, weapons, terrorists, and sex slaves in from Ontario. Also, we have looked into the financial dealings of certain individuals with regard to other services they may provide to willing customers."

"So, the money from Iraq has ended up in Pantherville in the hands of Chinese smugglers by coming through Ontario?" Rad asked.

"That's about the size of it, right now."

Bill Cote launched into a proposal to get Joe and Rad involved in option trading, but while he was explaining puts and calls, Joe excused himself by saying that he had an appointment to get all his teeth pulled.

"A full mouth extraction? I didn't know you rubbed snuff." Bill Cote was disappointed. He had more to say.

Walking out to the Malibu, Rad asked, "Are you really going to the dentist?"

"I was just stating one of the things I'd rather do than listen to Cote. I could have mentioned sleeping in a roadside ditch or fighting a shark with a toothpick."

Chapter 19

Sept 20

This was the third time this year that Joe had witnessed a parade of officials all making irrelevant noises, important to them, irritating to others. He had been talking to Brad and Ray, the marina's owners, in their boat showroom. They were in the parts area, near the offices, and nobody knew what they were going to do about Cletus, Hurricane Cletus that was.

The third hurricane of the season had tracked well to the west of the normal east coast path and come up through Ohio before swinging east down the lake. This had caused deluge-rains in Ohio, Pennsylvania, New York, and Ontario, swelling every feeder stream, creek, river, and rill on both sides of the lake. The powerful rain had scoured the streams of wood such as logs, trees, and everything that would float and many things that didn't float. Natural currents sent them downwind to the Musky Straits. Looking out the window at the marina's work slip, Joe could see a shopping cart, an overstuffed love seat, and the remnants of the steel cab of a pickup truck resting atop the solid mass of floating wood that blanketed the water's surface.

The Musky Straits wasn't technically a river, having neither source nor mouth. It was a strait, a narrow passage between two large bodies of water. But, it acted like a river with current and back eddies because of the drop in elevation of two hundred forty feet, over a short stretch of twelve miles. Here at the Royal Marina, the river came into a back eddy behind the breakwall that protected the north, or down-bound, end of the single navigation lock operated by the US Army Corps of Engineers. The lock was constructed so commercial traffic could reach the towns between Pantherville and Cascades. The Red Rock Canal crossed under the highest arch of the Friendship Bridge in US waters so that large ships could travel under the bridge.

Local lore said that the border between the USA and Canada was determined by dropping a log into the water under the Friendship Bridge and tracking its progress as it floated downstream, in a northerly direction. That log had favored Canada so much that above Strand Island, where the Straits split to go around both sides of Big Island, the river was Canadian for seven eighths of its width. Any traffic up-bound in the river that did not use the lock was in Canada most of the time. This fact of geography had created an administrative nightmare after the attacks of September eleventh. As long as US-registered boats didn't touch land in Canada, they were ignored for Customs purposes, if they were not doing anything suspicious. The same was true regarding Canadian boats in US waters.

Joe Gaspe looked at a river clogged with floating debris, hundreds of tons of driftwood all the way across its two-mile width, but especially densely packed in the area above the lock, which was approximately the size of a football field. In normal times, every bit of crap in the river flowed into the back eddy and spent a few days or hours floating in circles until the lock's activity, or a wind shift, flushed it down-river.

"There's at least fifteen full-sized trees here in the docks," this, from Dan Prestle, the night watchman, irked Brad, the marina owner, who got a fair amount of mileage out of being grumpy.

"We've got to start pulling boats for customers," Ray said. He was the self-effacing partner with the full head of black hair that contrasted with Brad's baldness. Was it just Joe's imagination, or did all bald guys look mean?

"John and Josh are looking into a way to start clearing the slip. I've got a call in to the Army Corps. We'll have to see what happens." Brad said this in the direction of Joe Gaspe, who had said he wanted to get out for some musky fishing.

The clock had crawled past nine AM when the woman from the EPA came in wearing her yellow hardhat. There was no danger of anything falling on her in the marina showroom. She was the first of several who were to sport a plastic bump cap as the theme of the day.

"Hello. I'm Louise Brotmarkle from the Environmental Protection Agency. And you are? She projected her small hand to Joe Gaspe who jerked his thumb over his shoulder at Brad while saying, "Joe Gaspe, fisherman." Joe reached to shake her hand and she withdrew it, gave him an annoyed look and turned to Brad.

Brad looked at Ray with an expression that said, "Did you call these people?" and shook the lady's hand.

"I'm here to inform you that you cannot remove these objects from the river until we have inspected them for pollutants and foreign bodies." Joe was staring out the window at a great blue heron sitting on a waterlogged love seat floating on the mass of driftwood.

Brad and Ray had dealt with the EPA before and Ray took over, using his charm, trying to keep Brad's wrath in check. "We'll need to be pulling boats for winter storage in a few days. Can you tell us when you'll clear us to open up our work slip?"

"My job is to warn all the entities on the river that they cannot remove potentially hazardous materials until inspection occurs. Another person from the agency will contact you in about a week to set up an inspection schedule. Sign here," she held out a paper with white, yellow, and pink copies.

Brad was fuming now. "Lady, this is wood, logs and trees, what hazard?" Brad was interrupted when the door opened and a slick fellow in a green hard hat came in. The front of his bump cap said CBP on it.

"Are you in charge here?" This to Joe Gaspe with no handshake proffered. Joe rolled his eyes, jerked his thumb over his shoulder, and watched Brad simmer.

"It is my job to inform you that this debris must be removed in order to clear the border for immigration patrols. You have twenty four hours to remove all the debris from in front of this lock." The agent, who was too officious to introduce himself, held out a paper with white, green, and red copies.

Ray tentatively took the form and put on his half glasses to read it, when the door opened and the next hardhat came in. Though Brad and Ray knew several people at the U.S. Army Corps of Engineers (they provided excess parking for the corps employees on their property), this was a new guy wearing the olive drab bump cap with the Army COE logo emblazoned on it.

"I've been sent over from Musky County to inform you that we see no hazard to navigation here and we will not remove any debris except what is in the lock proper. When operation of the lock resumes we will expect you to prevent the influx of foreign matter during the up-bound operation of the lock."

"No hazard!!!" Brad was at a rolling boil now and Ray had a sickly green cast to his complexion.

"Since there is no commercial traffic on these waters there is deemed no hazard."

Joe wondered why the Army Corps was needed if there was nothing they could do.

"Sign here, please." The corps guy's manners were calculated to annoy. Ray set the paper, with its multiple copies, on the stack.

"How..." The door swung open and a man in an orange hardhat came in, followed by two uniformed officers, and followed by a man in a ball cap that said transit police.

"Hi, Joe Dombrowski. I've got a barge on the river with a crane and power shovel; I can..." This from the orange-hatted man, a burly guy with a puffy face and a classic whiskey nose.

"The Sheriff's boat must be able to transit this lock, you'll have to remove this debris right away." The Deputy Sheriff's statement was seconded by a Pantherville police officer that nodded his head as an example of city-county cooperation.

"We have to have the bus stop turnaround clear—don't be piling any of these logs in our right-of-way." The transit cop was pointing out the nearness of a major bus barn to the end of the marina's work slip.

Brad went into his office and slammed the door. Ray sputtered a response to someone. Everyone was talking at once when a Pantherville Fire Department official arrived and stated that the fire-boat must have access to the river through the lock. He stated this even though the end of the lock marked the end of Pantherville and the start of the suburb of Gunmore.

Ray kept getting greener, and his head was kept turning, watching all these hard hats talking at once, and each turning up the volume to be heard. Joe turned and looked at the massive clog of logs. He saw John and Josh backing a pontoon boat into the work slip with a jerry-rigged plow attached to one end of it. Brad appeared at the door of his office smiling, and waved Ray inside, closing the door.

Joe could see them inside the office, but could hear nothing. Brad made a point, Ray shrugged, Brad made another point, Ray raised his arms palms open, Brad finished, and reached for the doorknob, Ray nodded. The door opened and Brad came out into the crowd of jabbering officials.

"Your attention, please." The noise began to recede

"Your attention, please. If you will please place your papers in this pile, my partner and I will complete them and, as soon as our attorney has examined them, they will be returned to you. Thank you and good day." This brought forth some tut-tutting, and some noises of satisfaction, but the officials—slaves to paper that they were—complied and piled up their forms for completion. Those without papers, the two law-enforcement officials and the private contractor' hung back, waiting.

"I'm sure you ladies and gentlemen have more people to visit, so we won't keep you." Brad was in control now—something important to him in his shop—and had begun to smile in an evil way.

Joe turned back to the window where John and Josh had begun to push the logjam with the pontoon boat, making slow progress on the pile. All the stakeholders along the river reached the same conclusion that day, which was to ignore the meddling bureaucrats and push the debris into the current, letting the next guy downstream worry about it. For Regal Marina that would be a ten day task, as they continued to get backflow from the deadheads piled up in the lake, waiting for their turn to head downstream.

Joe walked out along the edge of the water. Brad, who drove up on a golf cart, joined him on the sea wall. "Look at that dumb bastard in the Cigarette boat," Joe stated this without glancing at Brad. A speedboat was flying along at full speed just beyond the floating island of wood.

"Somebody's shop is going to get some work when he trashes that out drive." Brad waited a second and then went on, "No illegals or troublemakers coming through here for the next few days. You'd think the Corps guys, who I work with, or the Border Patrol who I'm helping, would give me a break."

"Those guys are just bureaucrats—they service their paperwork—that's all. Besides, no one really knows the details of what we're doing. The less I tell them the better they like it," Joe didn't like talking about his network.

"Rad, I enjoy working with you and I'm convinced that you've changed my relationship with my daughter since we've been working together."

They were in the Malibu; Rad was driving Joe on his errands. "Are you drunk?" She looked out of the corner of her eye. Joe being touchy-feely just didn't seem right.

"No, no, sober as a judge er maybe not. I want to tell you that I like working with you and you've helped me get over my beliefs in what a girl could be. I'm telling you this because I am going to let you down.

" I think I've got this plot figured out and there is going to be a period of danger involved. I'm not going to put you at risk. Rudi

Loonch told me once that the problem with putting women in combat is not so much the behavior of women but the behavior of men when women are around."

"You know what the trouble with Uncle Rudi is? The most annoying thing is he's usually right." Rad had a fire in her eyes as she'd pulled over and was staring at Joe.

"Look, I'm gonna have a mission on the boat, I owe it to Marv to include him and you don't do well on the water. My mind is made up. I just didn't want you to think that your efforts haven't been appreciated."

"Just give me something to do in support."

"Okay, I can do that."

"We know who did the actual killing of Derek Chang now but we don't know the identity of the man behind the murder." Thomas Andre was being too revealing for Joe to be comfortable. Joe liked it better when he didn't reveal details and Andre offered little in return. His new life suited Joe Gaspe.

They were sitting on a park bench facing the moving waters, a mile wide, with Big Island across the Straits. Both men felt a degree of comfort when they watched the ever-changing water flow by, slate blue under the clouds, baby blue when the sun shone. They were in their third different venue for this discussion and Joe had convinced himself that Agent Andre, a man he considered untouchable, was worried about being watched and maybe he was even concerned about his safety.

Joe wasn't used to Agent Andre acting nervously. He had always been so self-assured, yet today he was looking over his shoulder a lot as they had their talk. At each little observation park along the Straits, there was an agent with a vehicle waiting for Andre to switch cars with him. Even with the switches Andre wouldn't talk in the vehicles, only when they were walking or sitting beside the rushing waters of the Strait.

"You found the killers but they won't talk?"

"They had been killed themselves, but we found forensic evidence from Derek Chang's murder which could only have been taken by the murderer. We are sure we have the right men. Two illegal Chinese immigrants. Huge, bulked-up, steroid monsters, from—this is for your ears only, Joe—the People's Liberation Army." Joe whistled softly. "What we don't know is who killed them. You remember the night you took that beating from the 'Arabs?'"

"How would I forget that? My knee's still killing me. And my shoulder. These Chicoms were in on that?"

"One of those fake Arabs was killed that night after being beaten with his own baseball bat." Joe nodded, remembering that. "Apparently, shortly after that, about a block away, these Chinese gentlemen were attacked and killed by unknown assailants. This happened in the concealed back parking lot of an empty warehouse building. The identity of their assailants is unknown. There was unique and conflicting forensic evidence at the scene of this crime. We have discouraged the Pantherville Police Department from too vigorous an investigation of the deaths."

A change came over Thomas Andre's face as he looked behind him. Joe glanced back as well and saw two roller bladers going in opposite directions, nothing unusual. He turned back to the water and a great blue heron winged slowly by, not fifteen feet in front of the bench they were seated upon.

"We need to move." Andre was firm but calm in his instruction. They walked toward the car they had been using but walked past it to a white Taurus. An FBI man got out of the Taurus, exchanged keys with Andre and went to the Impala Andre had been driving. They got in and Andre drove off down the Straits.

"Tell me about this unusual evidence," Joe said when they were on the road. Andre looked at Joe and shook his head. "I forget Joe, do you like the Yankees or hate them?" Joe didn't care about professional sports in the least, but recognized Andre's change to a subject so banal, as a hint that the car may not be clean.

At the next stop, the fourth of the Straits Stretches they'd been on, Joe and Andre strolled along a path to another bench.

"What's going on? Are you afraid of something? What was that unusual evidence you were about to tell me?" These rapid-fire questions were proof that Joe's nerves were on fire.

"Joe, a man in my position must be cautious. Don't be concerned, this is just tradecraft." Joe knew when someone was blowing smoke. He waited, watching the water, slightly stained here, just downstream from a feeder creek.

"The enhanced Chinese gentlemen were overpowered decisively by we don't know who or what. Joe, this is again ears only—there were three wild bird feathers at the scene—my scientists tell me one each from a raven, a hawk and a heron. There was a tuft of fur from a black bear on the fender of the car that contained one dead body, and…"

"Oyaron." Joe uttered that one word in Mohawk. Agent Andre looked at Gaspe with a quizzical expression.

"But the strangest thing was that they were scalped, expertly scalped I might add, and their throats were penetrated with a dagger so that they bled out. Lodged in the larynx at the bottom of one wound was the point of a heron's beak. The dagger used to finish them off was the beak of a great blue heron. Who would have one of those other than a Native American?"

Joe had closed his eyes at the last part of Andre's speech and he clearly saw Mo Snow nodding at him with three great birds perched above him. The revenge had been made possible because of the spirit animals of his clan. "You think they were killed by Indians?"

"Maybe it was like the Boston Tea Party, made to look like Indians."

"Yeah, that's probably right." Joe turned away and smiled to himself when another heron flapped its wings in a slow ascent into the wind.

"Did you ever find anything out about that boat that caused the ruckus on Labor Day?" Joe wanted to change the subject. He knew, or thought he knew what happened to the Chicom bodyguards. Mo's involvement was one of those details Thomas Andre didn't need to know.

"I am awaiting a report from the authorities in Ottawa on what they learned about that reckless pilot, as you called him. I am a patient man."

"You'd better be patient if you are waiting for the Canadians to voluntarily give anything up." Joe still had some resentment for his friends from the north.

Andre looked calmly at Joe and didn't rise to the bait.

"I think there are a lot of people in the government up there that don't wish us well. Some of them hate the US so much they'd like to see the terrorists win. I'm not so sure that all of our own people are on our side. In fact, my partner Rudyard thinks the CIA tried a coup and failed. Whattya think, are the CIA goons working for the dark side?" Joe was ranting but felt like he was on a roll. Why stop?

"The government of Canada is a vital ally of the United States of America. The CIA and FBI have been charged to work together in the Department of Homeland Security. Is every individual to be relied on? No, I don't think so. But the leadership is totally reliable." Andre repeated the company line.

Reading between the lines, Joe began to grasp why they'd been shuffling vehicles and moving around. He took a flyer at defining the problem. "The reckless pilot incident was a practice attack on the USA coming from inside Canada—not by Canadians but by terrorists who move freely within Canada. The report will be stepped on so many times it will be a year late and totally empty of content. Nothing has been done to stop a real attempt on the bridge." Joe was wound up now. "On top of that, you are in danger from elements within Homeland Security who want you, not only to fail, but to disappear!" Joe stared at Assistant Special Agent in Charge of the Pantherville Office of the FBI Thomas Andre. He tried to read in his expression an answer to his expressed scenario.

Thomas Andre had an entirely bland look on his face with his eyes fixed on a spot in the middle distance. He nodded once.

❈

Some ideas took a long time to settle down in Joe Gaspe's mind. They were there, but they had no context, didn't tie in with other ideas, and Joe just forgot about them. Then at an odd moment, one of those ideas would roll up against another one, stick to it, and together they'd form a new concept for Joe. When he was working in his shop, turning wooden fishing rod handles on his lathe, gluing up or clamping his bamboo rod pieces, or staining and varnishing those handles, or when he was painting fishing lures for his buddies, wrapped up in the physical and precise nature of his work, some things would click together and he'd jump to write them down or they would go back to rolling around. He had never been one to grasp concepts quickly. His mind was a riot of chaotic information from his senses. He had excellent but untrained vision, he could recognize odors but not sort them out, and he thought he was crazy because he could feel things empathically that were happening to others. Those were his Mohawk senses. On his Irish side he was an enthusiast of tastes and he heard things in mystic dreamy languages that he did not speak but unaccountably understood. He had never tried to rein in his senses. He only indulged himself as far as it was legal, but he also struggled against a darkness that he knew was in him. Part Mohawk, he could sit and stare at a fire for a month in contemplation, but part wild Irish tribesman, he felt a goad pushing him to leap, and howl, and flit about.

High School had been hell for him and without the extra credit that he had earned by being the de facto teacher in the woodshop and paint shop and carpentry classes, he'd never have made it out. Back in those days, you could pass a grade by taking one test. He'd gotten through algebra, Spanish, French, and English classes with the help of a crib sheet given him by a teacher—a former priest—who recognized an individual, talented with his hands, on whom an academic education would be wasted.

Joe's rod shop was his refuge from a house full of women. He could create what he wanted, experiment as he liked, and succeed or fail on his own. He was a craftsman and not a businessman. He never charged enough money for his products. He always had too many unused materials. He created items that had no value outside of the challenge involved in creating them. He didn't promote his products in ways that would make them known to potential customers. He had to hold down a full time job as a carpenter and take side jobs for cash. He was still broke most of the time.

It was in the shop that he felt that he could control the rage that was within him. By working, thinking, writing down his deductions, reading snatches of his few favorite books, and returning to his craftsmanship, he could sort out ideas. Using his hands, exploiting his skills, and letting that mind of his be free to chew over those ideas until they rolled into some pattern, he reached understanding. Even now, being well paid for his work for Thomas Andre, he needed the time in his shop to be right with the world. What had his partner Rudyard called it? "Ordering his universe."

He was down there turning a piece of cherry for a second fly rod ordered by Thomas Andre, when he began to feel very strange. At first, he wouldn't recognize the feeling. He thought he had to pee but when he went he only produced a dribble. Then he thought maybe he was feeling pressure, as they say. But he'd made love to Kate last night in a burst of pent up ecstasy for both of them. Busy married people, with jobs, and kids, and money issues, had trouble finding time for each other. Then he thought maybe he was constipated but that wasn't it either. He turned off the lathe and went to the stool by the coffee pot and poured himself a cup.

Marv wasn't around, nor were any of the other guys who'd occasionally hang around the shop drinking beer and watching him work. Then, as he set the coffee cup down, those ball bearings, that were his unconnected thoughts, started to bunch up in one corner of the milk jug that was his mind. Mel Dumke was buying boats for somebody in Canada. One of those boats had behaved strangely near the Friendship Bridge. Dumke was helping to smuggle Chinese people from Canada to the USA. The killers of Derek Chang had been Chicoms. The owners of Dumke's landscape business were probably Chicoms, hidden by a few false front companies.

Thomas Andre had said that if the plot were hatched entirely in Canada, the State Department or CIA would have to deal with the

Canadians. He also had hinted that those agencies were riddled with traitors. The $50 bill had been planted with terrorists in Iraq, as Bill Cote had told him.

Then, there was what Rudyard had said, "The Islamofascists have such contempt for our culture that they fail to pay enough attention in order to get things right. When told to send anthrax spores to the American Media, meaning the TV networks, *Washington Post,* or *New York Times,* they had looked up American Media on the Internet and come up with a minor player in Florida called, American Media—publisher of the *National Enquirer*—and attacked there.

There was that dream of the boats, held by grapnels, hurtling toward the bridge. And there were those warnings in his dreams. How could he honor those dreams? Then there was Dumke bragging about a holiday attack. Andre's Yemeni sources had said a holiday was involved, too. What if they got that wrong as well?

Joe sat with a cigarette and a cup of coffee and pondered the different paths taken by he and Mel Dumke. Both had been hammered by the upstate economy. Those businesses that didn't shut down entirely were purchased, stripped of their processes and systems, and shut down or moved to Mexico eventually. A lot of people were permanently laid off.

Why was Dumke filled with the poison of resentment while Joe and others moved on, made do, started over? Neither was a man of illusions but Mel Dumke saw the world through his own bitterness, frustrated desires, thwarted ambitions, and fear. Sure, Joe was afraid sometimes that his girls and wife might suffer, but then he took on more side jobs, worked harder, that's what a man did.

There's no special good fortune in store for any man. A man must make his breaks. He must find his way. He has freedom to be a great success but equal freedom to fail again and again. Joe could understand why Dumke appealed to the terrorists as a tool. What Joe couldn't fathom was why the CIA used Dumke. But he was more than ever convinced that they did. How else to explain his freedom to flit around, stinging like a mosquito?

Long ago he had learned that when the ideas, those ball bearings, all got stuck together in one corner of that milk jug, he needed to act on the issue. Once he'd solved the problem he had the mischief in him, and he had the rage to do something to upset the plans of others.

That was it. Joe knew what was going to happen. He dropped his cup, left the light on, went to the phone, and called Marv's cell phone.

Chapter 20

October 12th

The weekend of October twelfth, Canadian Thanksgiving, was when the yearly troll around the island took place. It wasn't quite an annual event since the four participating boats had only done it once, the year before. It combined a fishing tournament with a race and was geared towards fun and competition. Joe and Marv were the defending champions and looked forward to the event in their new boat.

The troll was arranged so that, if any musky were caught, by anyone, a team that merely sped around to win the race would not win the tournament. Each participating boat was provided with a disposable digital camera, one that included a date and time stamp on all the pictures. All muskies caught were to be photographed. They were required to take a picture in front of several waypoints. One crewmember had to be on shore for the photo, with the exception of the waypoint at Ensign Island, which was off limits to people. There, a date stamped photo of the "no landing" sign was required. Though it was called a troll, any legal method of angling was permitted.

In the previous year's competition Joe And Marv had won by three points, winning one leg of the race portion, and tying for most muskies caught with three, for a total of 93 points. JohnJohn and Clem had caught the biggest musky and one other for 80 points but had won no race legs.

Ozzy and Stryker had given up fishing, considered it only a race and had won four legs of the race, totaling 22 points. They had cynically guessed that nobody would catch any fish. Melvin and Snooky had caught three small muskies, for ninety points, but won no legs, leaving them three points behind Joe and Marv.

Marv was not pleased when Joe told him that they were not going to compete this year. Joe broke the news to Marv right after the start of the race. He allowed the other boats to speed off while he headed in the wrong direction. Marv resigned himself to humoring the captain while at sea. Instead of starting the troll, Joe took Marv out into the lake to lurk in the Rainbow Channel. There they were to wait for one of two suspicious boats from Canada that, Joe said, planned to crash into the bridge. They bobbed on the current, waiting to see what was going to happen.

Joe explained his deductions to Marv as they drifted with both engines idling. "This is the time when I, we, have to do something. We can't hide from this. We've gotta take initiative or it will be taken from us. We've gotta be prepared. We are old enough to know that nothing is as easy as it ought to be, that we've got only so many chances to make a difference, that it isn't likely to get easier."

It's hard to sit waiting to spring a trap. Being ready all the time for instant action gets on one's nerves and lengthens the needed reaction time. They listened to the radio chatter from the participants in the troll. Marv asked questions.

"How do you know it's today? Why not just call your little black buddy and be done with it? How will we know the boat we're looking for? What's a fireship anyway?" Marv bored his eyes into him, leaned forward, and placed his hands on his knees, elbows out.

Joe had never considered himself a hero. He wasn't really sure why he was taking on an especially dangerous mission today. He didn't keep secrets from Marv, but how could he tell him that it was a bear in a dream that had propelled him into action? He had developed the plan, followed it to the logical conclusion, and only now, while they waited, did it dawn on him that they were the guys risking their lives. His heart thumped in his chest, he sipped coffee from his thermos, but his mouth remained dry.

Joe took the last question first. "Sometimes these were called block ships or, in the days of wooden ships, fireships. The one we're going to intercept is actually a floating bomb—bomb ships were platforms for heavy mortars. It will be used like a missile to blow up the Friendship Bridge."

Marv waved his left hand into the air, "I liked you better when you didn't know anything."

Marv challenged again. "C'mon, tough guy, if you've got a plan, are you gonna tell it to me before they get here?"

Joe looked at his partner with appreciation. The corners of his mouth smiled slightly. His eyes lit up.

"Do you think this is funny? Do these bastards expect us? Do they have guns?" Marv was unrelenting.

"They don't expect us. They won't have guns, I don't think. Here's what I'm gonna do. The pilot won't be an experienced boater, I don't think. He made a trial run to time his approach back on Labor Day. I'm going to mess up his timing. That big tub of a Coastliner 32 will wallow like a barge. I'm going to get inside of him, push him away from the bridge. Then I'm going to do a bat turn under the bridge and come back up between him and the abutment. Use my wake to push him out. I hope that will be enough impetus to force him into the middle. Here." Joe handed Marv a life jacket.

'So, when the bomb blows, we'll be between the bridge and the explosion. Been nice knowing you." Marv's displeasure was deliberate.

"Hopefully, the timing will get screwed up by our antics and they will mess up. Once past the bridge, they won't be able to get back to it. If they blow before the bridge...well, I hope they don't. If we can push them into the middle of the center arch, before it blows, I'll punch the throttles and we'll both pray."

"Kind of late for two guys like us to get religion, dontcha think?"

Joe smirked, chuckled, and handed his partner a photo of two Coastliners, a 32 and a 21, with silhouettes taped on the back. "One of those is what we're looking for. It will come from the lake—from the Canadian side—and hit the bridge. If the sun is behind them you can see the shape. But, that won't be until afternoon. They probably won't wait that long."

"Agent Andre knows my theory, I woke him at four this morning before we drove over. He's semi-convinced, I guess. The fact that everything will happen in Canada, until they are right under the bridge, is a big problem for him. He might be able to organize the Coast Guard, Sheriff, Army and all that for a threat in the US but the CIA gets the ball when the game is foreign. Organizing the Canadians is another matter. He's not confident. So we're here."

"Do you want to die a hero?"

"I don't want to die at all. We are going to do this." He emphasized each word by pointing down at the boat and tapping the wheel with his finger.

"I've been studying on this problem for four months. All that driving around with Radleigh, checking things out, has shown me stuff. I know you don't like this, but my dreams have pointed the way. There has been a lot of intelligence that I have gathered. Don't laugh. All this information has come together. That, and the realization that I am the only one who can do this, that's why we're here." Joe could have dwelled on his dreams but now was not the time to try convincing Marv that he believed that if he dreamed something, it would soon come to pass.

With time left, Joe thought over his plan one more time. Truth to tell, he couldn't concentrate on the plan. His mouth tasted like he'd bitten into a penny. His hands were tight on the wheel even though the boat was only floating. The October morning was brilliant, clear, and bright. There was no heat. no haze, no clouds. This was perfect weather for a northern man. The lake was fresh without any fishy odor. Only the faint oily smell of his motor tickled the edge of his sense of smell.

Rad was pacing back and forth at the gas dock at Royal Marina. It was where she got the best reception and she'd had several cell phone calls to make. She had called: her boss Mr. Hilliard of the Border Patrol, the Corps of Engineers, the Coast Guard, the FBI—Agent Andre— and the County Sheriff's office. She was trying to get someone to move on this threat that Joe saw coming and that no one else, with the exception of Andre, took seriously.

She looked at her phone, in that way cell phone owners have, of trying to will it to ring. A call came in. It was Joe's wife—Rad had forgotten that she had called her—trying to find out why she should be in Pantherville this afternoon.

Rad convinced her to show up without being specific about Joe's risky behavior. Kate thought she was coming to a special picnic or barbecue.

Rad continued to pace, trying to determine in her mind, by practicing quotes she would use, how to convince hardheaded stolid bureaucrats that they should react with decisiveness to the dreams of a crazy half-Indian half-Irish mystic.

"Nut job, more like," she said aloud to herself as her attention was distracted by a Lund pulling up next to the gas dock.

She glanced over to see Mo Snow, idling beside the dock. "Hello, Radleigh." He reached out and held the boat easily as it bobbed beside the dock.

"Mo, Joe is trying to stop an attack on the bridge! He's sure it's today. I'm scared. He and Marv are up in the lake looking for a boat that is nothing but a floating bomb!"

"Are you trying to get help?" He looked at the phone in her hand.

"Yes, but no one is taking this seriously. Joe thinks the terrorists, based in Canada, have the plan set for Canadian Thanksgiving instead of American Thanksgiving."

"Ah, that cousin of mine sees true. Keep up your trying. My helpers and I will see what we can do." Mo pushed off and headed into the river.

"Helpers?" Rad wondered, "He was alone." Rad returned her gaze to the phone and resumed pacing.

In the Boston Whaler, Joe and Marv sat and smoked in silence for what seemed like a long hour. Ozzy and JohnJohn were talking, boat-to-boat, on the VHF. Both were fishing near the power plant. The whereabouts of Melvin and Snooky was unknown. The tournament trollers weren't aware that Joe and Marv were not on the troll.

A thirty-footer, fully enclosed in canvas, with the heat on, came roaring up to the lake throwing a four-foot wake as it passed. The Whaler took the wake and Joe caught a glimpse of something to the west, crossing a shaft of sunlight. He slapped his binoculars to his eyes.

"Marv! Look off of the point." Marv's end of the boat came up as Joe's end rocked down. "Do you see somebody coming our way?"

"Yeah. There's one coming. Think he's our man?"

Joe stood after the wake had passed. He was not used to field glasses and it took him several seconds to find the boat and concentrate on it. It looked like the one. Marv studied the picture and flipped to the side with the silhouette. His head went up and down looking from boat to paper. Then, that nodding became accentuated, and he said. "I believe it is, Joe. The thirty-two footer is coming, now's our chance."

Marv stared at the oncoming boat. The Coastliner 32 grew in size as it approached. Joe looked at Marv, intently watching. Joe considered his partner. Marv was a bulldog once he got a grip on something and he wasn't going to let go. He was annoying sometimes, but who wasn't? In that way men have with their friends, Joe found Marv's foibles bothersome, but his overall attitude toward Marv was acceptance, loyalty, and confidence, even affection.

Joe considered how different it was with his wife. Home was a safe harbor where he could be accepted, not challenged. A man wanted loyalty, admiration, and appreciation, whether he deserved it or not. Why was it so hard to get those things? He went on adventures. He did heroic deeds. He turned in all his pay. Why couldn't he come home once in a while for a short spell of quiet and peace? Soon enough he'd have to go out and fight wars again.

Marv began to get excited. Joe calmed down, swallowed a big lump in his throat, closed his eyes in prayer, and handed the binoculars to Marv. "Hold these, gimme your cell, I'm going to try Andre once more."

The familiar voice mail prompt came on after one ring and Joe left a message, "Hey, Tom, this is Gaspe. It is coming down right now. I've got 9:15 on my watch. He's in Canada. I am, too. We are going to stop this. I hope." He disconnected.

Marv watched the boat with the binoculars. Joe put on his life-jacket and prodded the one in front of Marv, hoping he'd wear it. There was almost no time left.

On Canadian Thanksgiving, the Friendship Bridge is loaded with cars. Mostly, they contain Canadians heading east to spend their money shopping in the United States. It was a classic example of Arab terrorists misjudging the situation through arrogance and disdain for the culture they wished to destroy. They assumed that the infidels of Canada and those of the United States, being Christians, celebrated the same holidays. They were five weeks early for Thanksgiving in the US, but the threat to the bridge was still huge. Mostly Canadians— people the Isamofascists considered irrelevant and beneath contempt, but not the main target—would die instead of the son of pigs and monkeys that they considered Americans to be.

Joe had deduced that the second Monday in October would be the day of the attack by the Fireship, not the last Thursday in November. The Coast Guard insisted, from their reliable source in the Yemeni community near Pantherville, that it would happen in November. Marv hadn't been able to figure out exactly where Joe got his information though he knew many of those in his network. But eventually he had come to the realization that Joe's dope was good.

The Coastliner 32, its cabin loaded with a massive TATP fertilizer bomb—as used in Oklahoma City—had been drifting on the

Canadian side of the calm Upper Lake for the past twenty hours. Hassan and Tariq had prayed, waited for the cell phone call telling them to proceed, and tried to keep their nervousness at bay. At ten AM the call came and the familiar voice said, "Allah hu Akbar." They were to proceed. It was a six-mile run to the bridge abutment that was the only waypoint on their GPS. The Coastliner wallowed along at twenty miles per hour with its cabin overloaded. Hassan drove and Tariq would activate the timer with one mile to go. Both were prepared to die for the jihad.

Joe had surprised himself often enough. Despite an overall lack of good judgment, he had confidence, because he knew he was a good man in a crisis. It was a vision thing. When events seemed to happen faster and faster, his ability to see slowed down. Instead of film reeling past, he saw pages being turned. That's how it was now as he contemplated racing his boat to get it past the fireship and between the enemy Coastliner and the bridge. Because the cabin cruiser was so slow, he knew he could push it out of line with his wake, twice. His ability to concentrate was also a type of tunnel vision wherein he was only dimly aware of anything other than the fireship he was attempting to outmaneuver, and barely noticed his sidekick Marv as he moved around the boat searching storage lockers.

The Coastliner 32 turned through an arc to port as Joe and Marv picked up the sound of her noisy stern drives roaring at full throttle.

"He's got his throttles pegged, he'll blow his engine that way," Joe shouted as he ramped up his speed to begin the risky maneuver that he'd planned.

"He probably doesn't care." Marv grinned.

Hassan, whose faith had been judged more pure, knew that the buoys in the Rainbow Channel would lead him to his goal. He was to pass a red buoy on his right at two miles above the bridge, a green buoy on his left one-mile above the bridge and plow into the right hand abutment of the center arch at full speed. His only other responsibility was to be sure Tariq activated the timer at the green buoy; it was timed to blow after three minutes. There were no wakes of lake bound cruisers to buffet the Coastliner as there had been on the practice run on Labor Day. Boat speed wasn't important until he reached the green buoy. Then he must keep the speed as indicated on the GPS, at twenty MPH. Hassan prayed, kept his eye on the faithless Tariq, and, due to inexperience, over-steered. On he went. He stared at his objective; the piling was under a bridge jammed with three lanes of cars and trucks. He alternated praying and shouting for death to the infidels.

Joe's concentration was on the speed of his boat, throttles ninety percent to the limit. He had the faster boat and quickly set an overtaking course. Because the Upper Lake is dumping millions of acre feet of water down the drain into the Straits, both boats would pick up a speed boost from the current of as much as eight miles per hour as they closed on the bridge. The pilot of the Coastliner 32 had not considered that imponderable speed boost, had never made a practice run when there was no traffic to experience the full down hill effect. Joe hoped he would set the timer to his bomb too late. Joe trained his eyes on the approaching bridge abutment.

The bobbing fireship was headed straight for a main support column of the Friendship Bridge. This would keep him in Canada until the last moment. Joe remembered the words of Ian Drakulitch, while looking from bridge to boat, to his tachometer, "Coastliners either bob like corks, when they are too small, or wallow like barges when they are too big. Their designs look right, but they're always off a little, they suck in performance."

At the green buoy, Tariq flipped the switch on the timer. Hassan jammed both throttles hard though they didn't move and he added no speed. He bored in on his target. Hassan was startled by a shout from Tariq. He looked to see a faster boat gaining on them from behind. Hassan ignored this, thinking the infidel must be crazy. The time ticked away. Hassan headed toward the abutment. His engines screamed.

Joe steered his boat to come within inches of the fireship. He didn't want to hit it but he wouldn't have risked his hand between the boats. He raced past, and heard Marv shouting at the men in the other boat. He looked right into the eyes, dead eyes, of the other pilot. As soon as his stern cleared the bow of the Coastliner, Joe's wake pushed the bow of the bigger boat away from the bridge.

The infidel's boat passed between Hassan and the bridge, pushing him away from his goal. The wake from the speeding boat, inches away, pointed his bow in the wrong direction. When Hassan saw his mission slipping away, his inexperience made him do things that made him go further wrong. He over-steered in an attempt to correct his heading.

Joe passed the targeted bridge piling within inches, slammed his wheel to port as soon as his stern was beyond the stone abutment, fought the sucking action of the eddy below the piling, and slammed into a trooper-turn to head back up, nearly scraping the abutment on his port side.

Hassan did not know what to do. The other boat, that shouldn't have been there, turned and headed back toward him on a collision course with the Coastliner 32. Then Hassan turned the wheel the wrong way before realizing his mistake. The Coastliner's bow spun away from the bridge piling he was supposed to hit.

Marv and Joe had their blood up. Both were screaming unintelligible war cries. Grinning like maniacs they clipped the stern of the bigger boat with their bow pulpit, heard a sickening snap as the front rail splintered, saw the pilot of the other boat turning the wheel back and forth. And heard what they thought was the explosion. Joe leaned into the throttles, already at their limit, and headed away, toward the Upper Lake.

The timer activated the detonator; the explosion began with a blinding flash of phosphorous and a whooshing sound like a jet plane taking off. Hassan praised Allah when he heard a loud bang. The bang was the blasting cap. A cloud of smoke billowed from the cabin, filled the cockpit, and lifted into the sky. The boat didn't explode. It spun out of control. The engines stalled. The cabin windows under the bow blew out, emitting clouds of thick white, then yellow, smoke. The backwash eddy, past the abutment, sucked in the Coastliner and it sat there, twenty yards downstream from the bridge, burning and spinning slowly around. The overwhelming smell of sulfur, carried by the yellow smoke, filled the Straits from shore to shore.

The Coastliner spun out of the back eddy and began to float downstream with the current. All that was visible was the stern. The rest of the boat was under an enormous billowing smoke cloud. The Coastliner burned with flames hot enough to melt its aluminum railings.

Two hundred yards above the bridge Joe idled his motors and looked back.

"It's a fizzer! Thank God it didn't blow!" Joe smiled. Marv was mesmerized, watching the cabin cruiser slowly float into the Ontario side of the Straits and rapidly burn to the waterline. Two people dived into the water, one and then the other. They swam towards Canada unnoticed by the watchers from the bridge.

"That's some fire and brimstone there," said Joe.

"I've always wondered, what's brimstone?"

"Sulfur, Marv. Surely you smell the sulfur."

Joe and Marv high-fived each other, because they had won and because they were alive. Marv howled, hooted, and yelled, "All right!"

Mo piloted the Lund through the cloud of yellow smoke that was drifting toward the United States and continued upstream. He was looking for Joe's boat. He looked up to see a raven sitting on a cross-member of the bridge. The arrival of the raven indicated that all was not well.

The traffic on the bridge stopped when the sulfur cloud erupted. Tollbooths at both ends shut down leaving all the vehicles on the bridge stranded. Sirens wailed, horns honked, people shouted, some out of their cars looking at the burning boat, others in their cars trying to will the traffic out of their way. Authorities at both borders, worried that a car bomb might be on the bridge, awaited orders.

Joe relaxed his shoulders. He had not realized how tense he'd been. Marv was jumping around; his adrenalin rush had made him high as a mountaintop.

"We did it! We saved the bridge." Marv beamed.

Joe slumped in the pilot's seat, closed his eyes, and slowed his breathing. This made up for all the setbacks, layoffs, firings, evictions, and trouble with cops. That was all nothing now. He'd done something big. Really big. No one would ever know but he and Marv and Rad. Still.

His eyes flew open. The croak of the raven stirred him. Then a great blue heron flew past them, its long flapping wings were stirring the air.

"Marv! Something's wrong! Mo just told me."

Marv looked at his partner, frowned and turned back toward the lake. "Maybe that's the problem," he said pointing. It was the other boat Dumke had purchased, the Coastliner 21.

It was coming at full throttle toward the same abutment. Joe, dead in the water, saw it was going to pass him in no time. He ramped his twin screws and turned in pursuit.

Knowing from the drunken ravings of Mel Dumke that the second fireship was a twenty-one foot Coastliner, Gaspe had found out from Ian D that the boat only had one 170 hp I/O and would not be able to develop the speed of the Whaler's twin 185 hp Mercury outboards. In addition, Joe's boat rode better on plane, so he was able to close the distance steadily after he'd been passed by the new fireship. This twenty-one footer was riding high in the turbulence caused by the narrowing of the Straits. Enhanced by narrowing at the seven bridge pilings, the current in the Musky Straits picked up speed above the bridge.

Led by his friend the great blue heron, which was easily keeping pace with his speed, Gaspe had a sublime confidence as he hurtled after the fireship. As he had done with the first boat, he was going to get between the Coastliner and the bridge by going below it and roaring back inches from the abutment and using his wake to buffet the Coastliner away from the bridge. He hoped he could make the interdiction in time. Marv, loyal to a fault, never had the advantage of Gaspe's vision of the future.

People on the bridge, pointing at the boats below, were sure a second boat was attacking the bridge and they could not move. Some ran toward the US. Some ran toward Canada. Some screamed in terror.

Aboard the Coastliner, Mahmoud held the wheel, prayed to Allah for Godspeed, and steeled his nerves with his belief in Paradise. Abdul, a foil in the bomb plot, was the man who had purchased the two Coastliners. The first has been a 32 foot cabin cruiser that wallowed so badly that Hassan had missed the bridge by ten feet, grounded on the Canadian side, and burned, as the bomb—a sure thing from Ali of Montreal—had turned into a fizzer, burning the boat to the waterline. Tariq and Hassan swam to shore, and walked away. Tariq, who had to complete this mission to save his children in Pakistan from rape and torture and death, didn't know that they'd already been sent down that road. The torture was underway as he attempted to fulfill his mission.

There were four men praying out there then. Joe Gaspe prayed for a chance to divert the fireship, while Marv Ankara said a prayer of his own.

Gaspe's Whaler easily overtook the Coastliner in the race to the abutment and for the first time Mahmoud saw the other boat. He shouted, "Infidel! Abdul, shoot the crazy Infidel." Abdul was kneeling on the deck, praying as fast as he could. Mahmoud looked over again and saw Gaspe looking at him with his big shaggy head, face contorted in a scream of rage. He saw another man, Marv, pointing a gun at him and yelled once more for Abdul to get up and shoot the crazy Americans. Abdul continued to pray.

Marv aimed and fired the Whaler's flare gun at the Coastliner as they passed.

Looking up to see a red-tailed hawk dive from the bridge high above toward the head of Mahmoud, Joe shot past the enemy boat and pulled another fast turn, one hundred eighty degrees back to the south, by slamming the wheel to starboard. The wheel jumped under his hand on the sudden turn, which rolled his boat onto its side within a half foot of its shipping water. The boat's turn sprayed white water into the air. He straightened the wheel and Joe, going south, missed the abutment by only inches. Joe laughed like a maniac.

The impending collision with the bridge had the opposite effect on Mahmoud that it had on Gaspe. Time seemed to speed up; noise multiplied into a roar of boat motors, rushing waters, his shouts to Abdul, Gaspe's rebel yell, and the pow-fzzzzt of Ankara's shot. It all blended into a high-pitched whine like that made by an electric motor about to blow apart.

Gaspe saw that he would get an additional boost from the permanent wake caused by the prow of the abutment, enhanced by his wake and the rebound wake of his downstream passage. That, and the Coastliner's own wake, pushed the fireship toward the center of the channel and bounced it away from the Whaler. The boats did not even touch each other. Joe wondered at the fact that there was no collision to sink his boat. The combined wakes tipped him to the starboard side, eighty plus degrees and the rebound wake, as well as the Coastliner's passage so close beside him, dropped him back eighty degrees to port. They were tipped to within an inch of turning turtle but the boat righted herself. Joe roared back south, hoping to avoid the explosion.

Mahmoud had lost control of the Coastliner 21. It turned sharply to port and was pulled into the downstream back eddy, behind the abutment, where it began to drift in a slow circle downstream.

"Yee-haw!" shouted Marv as Joe looked at him, they high-fived, and they turned back to see one Arab jump into the Straits. The fireship ended its bobbing drift with a detonation like a mountain breaking in half and exploded into a huge orange fireball. It was the loudest sound either of them had ever heard. A yellow cloud soon replaced the orange flames. There was no more Coastliner 21, only a rain of debris.

Joe turned to look at Marv, saw the fireball reflected in his sunglasses, and felt the heat wave on his back. "I thought those rag heads were supposed to be suicide bombers."

"That SOB probably had to cool off a little, I shot a flare into his praying ass just as we went by them."

"You idiot, you could have blown us up, too!"

"As if you didn't put us in danger getting between a bomb and a bridge! Twice!"

At that point both Gaspe and Marv broke into hysterical laughter. Sirens began to wail in both countries and every law enforcement agency imaginable sent crews into action.

"Let's make ourselves scarce. I don't want to answer questions." Joe sidled the boat at trolling speed over towards the US side of the Straits. Marv set out two rods in trolling position and, in mere moments, they were just two musky fishermen heading home on one last run to the marina.

When they pulled into the boathouse, Joe didn't expect the lights and music to be on. He was equally surprised to see his wife, oldest daughter, and youngest daughter come around the corner.

Rad was there too, and they were cooking up some sausages, burgers and hot dogs. They'd laid out a picnic spread, apparently confident that the mission would succeed, and the boys would return. Joe hopped onto the dock and smiled weakly at Kate. She handed him a drink.

"Take this Joe, it's Rad's recipe: the juice of a whole lime, three fingers of dark rum, and Vernor's Ginger Ale over ice. I've already had one."

"Yum. What's the occasion?"

"There are a few of us glad to see that you're alive and not under the water."

"Does that include you, Amy?" Joe looked sheepishly at his eldest daughter.

"What do you think, you crazy man?"

"Well, we might as well eat," Joe said as he handed Marv a sausage and grabbed one for himself.

Thomas Andre showed up alone. He had called Joe and arranged for a meeting at the Cormorant Island pier. He had told Joe that he wanted to clear up a few loose ends.

"Let's walk this way." In his gracious way, Agent Andre ushered Joe along the walkway that went beside the Straits, under the Friendship Bridge and up along the Upper Lake.

"Through a fortunate turn of events, a boat that was little more than a floating bomb destroyed itself without harming this vital link between our nations." He moved his arm toward the bridge above them where Joe saw a raven perched. The bird bobbed its head.

"There was only one innocent casualty. A man on the bridge leaped to his death. The heat of the fire melted the vinyl siding of Mr. Chu's Chinese restaurant in Ontario. A gentleman of interest was detained as he climbed, cold and wet, from the Straits about one mile downstream. He had been observed by some Canadian fishermen who alerted the OPP."

"The threat from the fireship has awakened several people, and agencies, on both sides of the border to the possibility of terror attacks arising in one country and being completed in the other. No one, other than you and me, knows whose actions averted this attack. No one needs to know. Will you communicate this to Marvin Ankara?"

"Uh, sure."

"Before you ask, I will tell you that Mel Dumke will remain in place for now. If he were taken out, to be replaced by an unknown successor, we would need to start our efforts from a distant place. That would be of no advantage to us."

Agent Andre was quiet as they walked along on another of those October days that are too pretty to believe. The sun shone warm, the air was perfectly clear with no heat haze, the blue sky dazzled. Joe looked over at Ontario, bucolic and attractive, without the noise, industry, and dirt so endemic to the US side of the Straits. He saw the black stained siding of Mr. Chu's, and asked the FBI man, "So, is my work for you done?"

"Oh no, Joe, not at all."

Handy Order Form

Postal orders:
All Esox Publications
P.O. Box 493
East Aurora, New York 14052
Fax orders: 716-655-2621   Phone Orders: 716-655-2621
Email orders: info@allesoxpublications.com
Website: AllEsoxPublications.com

Please send more information on Publications: Yes_____ No_____

Name: _____

Address: _____

City:_____State/Prov:_____ ZIP/Postal Code_____

Please send the following materials. I understand that I may return any of them for a full refund, for any reason, no questions asked.

Quantity	Title	Price	Total
_____	*Fireships & Brimstone*	$37.50 US	_____
_____	*The Accidental Musky*	$ 6.95 US	_____
_____	*The Quest for Girthra*	$16.95 US	_____
_____	*Becoming a Musky Hunter*	$14.95 US	_____
_____	Understanding River Muskellunge DVD:	$15.95 US	_____

Sales Tax: NYS residents add 8.25%..............._____
Shipping: U.S $4 (Can $5) for first item
$1 (Can $1.50) each add'l item......................_____
Total..._____

Payment: Check____ Credit Card_____Visa___ Mastercard____

Card Number _____

Name (print)_____Exp. Date_____

Signature_____